Call Me Priscilla

College life is so boring. It's not at all the way you might picture it. It's all work and no play. Sometimes I find myself wanting to quit and become a stripper. When I'm at work, I often daydream about becoming a stripper, making lots of money, getting attention from guys, pissing my parents off…but mostly I wonder what my stripper name would be. I can never think of the right stripper name. Candy? Conquest? Quicky? I like Quicky 'cause it reminds me of oatmeal.

Shit, oatmeal on table seven. The customer at table seven comes in every day. His name is Preston, and he always tells me he's going to take me away from "all this." What's "all this"? I don't know; I just go with it. He's a good-looking man, probably my father's age. He's five nine with brown hair he slicks back. He has the deepest brown eyes and thickest brown eyebrows. His smile is so warm, and there's a certain something about him. It's hard to pinpoint exactly what that is. But he's always dressed in the best suits. I do get annoyed with his constantly asking me out and my politely rejecting him, but he's a good tipper, so maybe one day persistence will pay off—but not today.

"Sorry it took so long today, Mr. Williams," I say without trying to sound like I'm flirting. Guys often think I'm flirting because of my high-pitched voice; it's something I wish I could control better.

"How many times must I ask you to call me 'Preston'?" he quips, as he awkwardly grazes my hands and I awkwardly move them to my pockets. He continues to tell me how he's going to woo me one day and ask my father for my hand in marriage. I don't see myself ever getting married, but I laugh it off, probably being mistaken for flirting once again. "You really like teasing me, don't you?" he asks seriously. As I fumble and am unable to really make out any words, he grabs my hands from my pockets and holds them awkwardly again. "I'm kidding, pretty girl," he says. I nervously smile and walk away.

My boss has warned me about him, claiming he's a womanizer. I tell her I'm not interested in him. I've never been interested in sex. I've had it, and it's OK, but if I never engage in sex again, it wouldn't bother me. I can take it or leave it. My boss is a big lady; she reminds me of me if I were fifty pounds heavier. I think she knows this and is secretly jealous. We have the same name—Mary—and she's always threatening to fire me but knows I have my regular customers who stay and order extra food just so I'll wait on them. She grabs me by the elbows and tells me I'm off of table seven for good. I stare at her, kind of confused and slightly in pain 'cause my elbow feels like it's about to fall off. She scolds me, "You flirt with the customers again and you're fired." I roll my eyes and walk away.

When I go out to the floor, of course Preston calls me over. As I glance back at Mary, I tell him Suzette is going to take over his table. He looks hurt but smiles and says, "That's a shame, Mary. You're the only reason I come in here," which makes me feel good. I don't get a lot of attention from men outside of work. I mean, my roommate, Gwen, is always telling me how pretty I'd be if I didn't wear oversize sweaters and combat boots every day. I rarely wear makeup, and my blond hair is lucky if it gets washed once a week. Plus messy buns are in, right? At work, though, we're forced to wear tight clothes, so I guess my inner tomboy can't be masked when my DD breasts are on display for the world. I hate my boobs; they hurt my back and make men act stupid. All my high school relationships were with guys who wanted to feel my boobs, so I stopped showing them off. Less attention from guys but also less drama. They're great, however, for being a stripper. See what I mean? Always back to stripping.

I've never even been in a strip club before. I'm a nineteen-year-old girl, and I've never set foot in one—is that weird? Probably. I wouldn't really know; my roommate thinks it's weird that I've never had my pussy eaten out before, so maybe I'm just inexperienced. I feel like my tits would make bank just by bouncing while I tried to dance. Maybe I can convince Gwen and her boyfriend, Diesel, to go with me. They probably wouldn't judge me since they're always talking about titty bars. Might be something fun for a Friday night. Maybe tonight!

By the time I get back to my dorm, Gwen and Diesel are getting it on, and it's only 10:00 p.m. It's awkward when I interrupt them but what am I suppose to do, stay at work all night? Go to the library on a Friday night? Gwen sits up, looking embarrassed, and Diesel tries to lift himself up but only manages to flop over Gwen's bare breasts. "You should really just join in with the timing you have," he says in a surprisingly nonjoking way. I roll my eyes while Gwen asks me what my plans are.

"You all wanna go to a strip club tonight"? I say, completely straight-faced.

Expressionless, they both stare at me then laugh. "Virgin Mary wants to get a lap dance?" Gwen mocks.

"Ha-ha. I'm not a virgin, bitch. I just thought it'd be fun. I've never been."

"Diesel isn't going anywhere near another naked girl as long as I live. I'm certainly not gonna pay for his broke ass to do it either," she barks.

Diesel looks at me, disappointed. Gwen isn't happy with his not backing her up. "You wouldn't want to go, right?" she threatens.

He shrugs. "Whatever. It could be fun. It could be kind of hot, baby… get me going for round two."

Gwen shoves him off her, stands up, and throws on a black slip from last night along with a pair of black stilettos. "You all go to the strip club and get fucked by a bunch of hos with herpes. I'm going to Greek row to get wasted." She slams the door shut, like the drama queen she is.

"You still wanna go?" Diesel asks me, completely exposed at this point.

"Um, no," I say, a little confused as to why he even asked me after Gwen epically blew the whole little idea out of proportion.

"Gwen is such a bitch. Everything has to be her way. She gets mad when I don't come inside her."

"TMI," I gripe, as I toss him his boxers.

"Don't like what you see?"

I mimic choking myself, as if the thought of having sex with him makes me want to regurgitate my eggs from dinner earlier, and hoping he gets the idea. In all honesty, he is very handsome. He's a total rich boy, with blond hair, blue eyes, a nice tan, toned calves, and a killer six-pack. I'd do him if he weren't Gwen's boyfriend, and if he didn't say such crude things. Plus, I don't know what he looks like erect, but his limp penis does nothing to get my girly parts tingling. Trying to snap myself back to the reality of my just wanting to go to sleep and get him out of here, I get short with him. "Well, bye."

Diesel comes up to me, towering over me at six three. He's a whole foot taller than me, and his chiseled shoulders are about twice my width. "Come on. Play nice," he says, as he runs his hands over the outside of my uniform, from my breasts, to my waist, down to my hips, pulling me into his pelvis.

"As if," I tell him. "You just fucked Gwen. And you're a pig."

"Cunt," he quips as he picks up his shirt to leave.

I've never been called a cunt before. The word strangely turns me on, though. I don't think about sex that much, but it's all I can think about throughout the night. I don't get off on masturbation, so unfortunately it's a sleepless night, but my God, do I want him. Gwen is a bitch; she probably wouldn't even care if I fucked Diesel. She fucked my first college boyfriend, so it would make it fair.

The next day I wake up to a skinny ginger passed out in Gwen's bed. It's 7:00 a.m.; Gwen can't already be up. Sure enough, I find her passed out in the bathroom in her own vomit. I don't have time for this right now. I have to be at work at ten and also try to squeeze in a two-hour library sesh before then. I throw on my cream cable-knit sweater over a flannel shirt with some denim shorts and of course my combat boots.

On campus I run into Diesel, who asks me if Gwen came home. I tell him no—she texted me last night that she was spending the night at the sorority house. He tells me I'm looking hot today, and I tell him to go to hell. Then he calls me a tease. Why do guys think I'm always teasing them? Is that their way of hoping I'm interested in them? I assure him that I'm not teasing. As I walk away, he shouts something about going to a strip club with him tonight then cackles hysterically. I ignore him and keep walking. For some reason his boyish laugh and joking manner isn't getting me excited. Why did he turn me on last night? Must have been from my lack of sleep, or maybe there was something off about those eggs Mary made me. Diesel is just so disgusting.

When I finally get to work at 10:05, Fat Mary yells at me again. What else is new? She screams at me that I'm late and that I need to put on some makeup 'cause I look tired as hell. Fat Mary's face is pretty; I don't know why she always has to be so grumpy. She probably needs to get laid.

Table seven walks in. It's eleven on a Saturday; it's not really like him to be here. Fat Mary sees him walk in and sends me on my break—how convenient. I can't even say hi to him. I go outside to get some fresh air and sit on the dirty corner, just to get off my feet, and put my head between my legs to get five minutes of rest. I've drifted off to sleep when I'm woken up by two guys yelling. One looks like he just got knocked out, and the other is trying to help him as they try to get away while maintaining their manly dignity from whatever just happened. They cuss and give the finger…to me? No. I look around, confused by the scene, and there I see table seven, shaking his fist. He sits down on the filthy street corner with me. Once he's seated, he holds his knees like I'm holding mine. "Haven't done that in a while. Hurts a little more than I remember," he says.

"What happened? I ask, genuinely perplexed by this whole chain of events, which couldn't have transpired over more than a three-minute time span.

"Just some boys trying to be all cool in front of their bros, who took off running the minute I grabbed the fag by his shirt."

I look at him, still confused, mouth open. He closes it for me and says some guys were taking pictures in front of me where my head was down to make it look like I was blowing them on the street. Who even does that? Boys. This is exactly why I don't date, period. That's exactly what I tell table seven too. He laughs and says I should try dating men instead of boys.

"Like you, Mr. Williams?" I whisper, fully intending to be flirtatious, as I'm still a little foggy from waking up.

"Preston," he bites back, as if I've offended him.

I shrug. "Whatever you want."

"Say that to me again." He looks me sternly in the eyes. His eyes are so cold but intense—wow. Maybe I'm the one who needs to get laid; I can't stop staring at his eyes.

Feeling confident, I grab his hands as he did mine the previous day. "Whatever you want," I tell him, and push myself up from the corner.

"Where are you going, young lady?" he calls after me.

"Back to work. Some of us have to make a living, Mr. Williams." I don't know where all this confidence is coming from. Maybe I'm just delusional and tired from this chaotic week filled with school, work, and family issues.

"Are you ever going to let me take you out, Mary?"

I pretend to ignore him when suddenly he blocks the restaurant's back entrance, preventing me from entering.

"Will you please stop teasing me and let me take you out?" he says. "Please. Let me take you on a proper date. You're not going to make me beg, are you? I'll take you anywhere you'd like. It's Saturday night. I'd love to take you to dinner."

I merely look at him, a million thoughts running through my head. He's handsome. Would he expect sex? What would I wear? He's old enough to be my father, which would piss my father off. I wish I had a second job as an excuse. A second job—that's my excuse!

"I'd love to, Mr. Williams, but I have to work tonight."

"The restaurant closes at ten."

"I…uh…have a second job," I say coyly. Did I just say that? Ugh. I don't have a second job. What's your second job, Mary?

"I didn't know you had another job. What is it?"

"It's kind of embarrassing. I don't want to say."

"Please tell me."

"I'm a stripper, OK? Work's slow, and I need money for tuition."

Where did that come from? I never lie, but suddenly I'm pulling a Gwen, making this up on the spot. Too many daydreams of being a stripper. Ugh, what's my stripper name? I spend all day thinking of the money and the boners I'd feel, but I don't even have a name.

"Oh, I see." Preston gives me a disappointed look.

"See why I can't go out with you now? Besides that, my boss would fire me if she found out."

"Which club?" he probes, as if he didn't hear what I just said.

Again, out of thin air, I pull out "Beavers' Damn, right by the airport." It's the only club I've seen, and I've only seen it while driving to and from LAX. "I gotta go back inside. Excuse me."

As Preston moves out of the way, I can feel his disappointment in me. I suppose that's what it would be like if I really did become a stripper—disappointed looks and shuns from random strangers. That also would mean my dad and mom would be disappointed in me. Then they might start feeling guilty about how they raised me, which might be worth it.

Ready to get back into something normal and familiar, I put on my apron when I hear someone screech my name from the back office. It's Fat Mary, looking extra fat in her blazer. "Mary," she says, "I've been waiting a long time to finally get this opportunity. You're fired."

My heart feels like it's being ripped out of my chest. My parents agreed to pay for half my college tuition only if I got a job to pay the other half. What am I supposed to do? Where will I go? I feel myself about to grovel and beg my boss to let me stay. Tears fill my eyes.

"Oh, poor, pretty Mary. Those blue eyes and pouty lips aren't gonna get you out of this one. I told you not to flirt with the customers."

"Preston?" I squeak out.

"Oh, you're on a first-name basis with him now, are you? I saw you two out back. I gave you warnings, missy. Get your things and leave now."

In shock, I stand there with uncontrollable tears pouring out of my eyes.

"Are you deaf or just dumb?" she says. "Let's go."

She grabs my elbow and leads me to the back. I get my purse and sweater, and she takes me through the dining area and strips my apron off me in front of everyone. At that point I run out of the restaurant as fast as I can. I stop in front of the bus station, behind the advertisements, to catch my breath. I feel like I'm having a panic attack. I can't get any air; I feel as if I'm about to die. My body shakes; my heart jitters; my eyes are so puffy that I can barely see. My knees buckle, and I fall to the ground. I sit on top of my cream sweater, with all the contents of my purse scattered around me. A man comes over, picks up the spilled items, and puts them back in my bag. I feel a little calmer when I look to see who it is. It's Preston. My calmness, however, immediately turns into embarrassment. My face turns bright red. I can't stand look at him. He offers to help me up, but I yell at him that I'm fine and tell him to leave me alone.

I go back to my dorm room to find Gwen and Diesel cuddling and being all lovey-dovey again. They can see I'm upset, but they don't care.

"You're not going to even ask what's wrong?" I scowl at Gwen, who's supposed to be my best friend.

"Oh, like you did this morning when I was choking on my own vomit?"

She's right; I didn't help her, but that was her own fault. What happened to me at the restaurant wasn't anything I brought on myself.

"I just…I just…had a…a…I just…" I can barely breathe through the anxiety. They both mock me. "Can't you both just give me a break? I just got fired!"

"Oh, Princess Mary isn't going to make hundred-dollar tips off old men getting off on her tits under their napkins during breakfast?"

"Ew. Really, Gwen? Diesel was right—you are a bitch"

"What's she talking about?" she says, shooting daggers toward her half-naked beau.

"Mary's crazy," Diesel says. "I don't know what she's talking about."

This isn't what I need after the morning I had. It isn't even noon yet, so I decide to leave my room and sit in the common area. I sit down there, staring at my phone for at least an hour, deciding whether I should call my parents to tell them what happened or call the restaurant and beg for my job back. I don't do either. My parents don't have to find out. With what they've put me through, they owe me half my tuition so I can try to do something with my life. Fat Mary was a bitch, the way she humiliated me in front of my regular customers. She probably got the biggest gleam of satisfaction out of that. In fact she's probably sitting in her office beaming that she's the only semi-attractive one there now under two hundred pounds.

Suddenly my mind drifts to my most frequent daydream, the strip club. Cherry? That could work; maybe I could wear red lipstick as my signature thing. After each dance I'd give the guys a kiss on the cheek to leave my red imprint on them. Where do strippers even buy those shoes? Maybe I'll go to Hollywood Boulevard. I remember seeing something like that when Gwen and I went Halloween shopping last year. My daydream eventually turns into an actual dream as I drift off to sleep, laying my head on my dirt-covered cream sweater, which is suddenly pulled from underneath me, giving me a massive headache as I hit my head on the common-room futon frame.

"What the fuck?" I shriek. Why's everyone waking me up today? Ugh, I dress like a homeless person so people will ignore me. I look up to see Gwen in Diesel's shirt.

"You tried to fuck my boyfriend?"

"What?" I say, confused.

She grabs my bun and slams my head into the same hard sofa edge I rebounded from seconds ago.

"You're a crazy bitch!" I scream. Then I feel her bare foot kick my head, and I fall to the floor. The dorm monitor breaks it up, along with another boy who's in the room. If they hadn't intervened, Gwen might have killed me.

"I'm moving in with Diesel. Good luck finding another roommate, bitch!" she says, as she tries to get her hair in some kind of order. Then she storms off.

I lost my job and my roommate, and now I have to go a hospital I can't afford. I can't even process what happened, and I don't even know what she said. I think it was something about Diesel.

I return to my dorm room with a bandage on my head and see that Gwen already has cleaned out her closet. Shit. She really is moving out. There's no way I'll be able to keep this place. One's life can change drastically in the course of twenty-four hours. Just yesterday I was complaining about how boring college life is. Now I wish it would go back to boring—something I know and something I feel safe with.

I crash out in my bed. When I wake up, it's already 11:00 p.m. I can't believe I slept that long. Furthermore I can't believe this whole day was real. I walk to the library—which is open all night—to start some early research on my term paper and try to gain control of something in my life. First I have to get some coffee if I'm going to actually get any work done.

When I enter the convenience store, I get some catcalls; I forgot I'm still wearing my work clothes. Cleavage really does make men stupid. One of them asks me, "How much?" Totally disgusted, I get my coffee and wait in line. I stare at the neon open sign for a few moments, while my admirers continue to taunt me, saying I'm a hooker. I turn around and snap into my best Gwen impersonation. "You want me? Come to Beavers' Damn tonight at midnight, and I'll get you and your little baby peckers off."

"Cunt!" the loud one hisses at me.

I don't know who I am; it's like I'm turning into a gremlin. I want to stab him with my heel. When I'm testifying in court, I can always blame it on my head trauma from earlier. I throw my hot coffee at his face and bolt for the exit. He and his friend run after me and grab me just as a police officer comes right through the door—perfect timing.

"Is there a problem here?" the cop questions, as if bored by the situation.

The two men let me go, and I leave. I walk a few blocks until I feel I'm a safe distance away from the convenience store and sit on the bus stop bench, trying to figure out what to do. Part of me wants to run away like in Saturday-night made-for-TV movies. Take a bus and just go anywhere. I wish I had the balls for that. I also wish my mom hadn't been such a goddamn alcoholic while I was growing up; otherwise I could go tie one on at the local bar like all my other peers who are going through shit. I can't stop thinking of the neon open sign and how pretty it is. I think the idea of being a stripper is glamorous, but I always feel bad taking money from lonely men. Then again lonely men are always taking away my self-worth and sense of safety just when I go to get a cup of coffee, so maybe that's the universe's way of evening the score. I run to a taxi up the street, get in, and ask the driver to take me to Beavers' Damn.

When I arrive at the club, I walk up to the entrance, where a bouncer stops me and says I have to pay. I tell him I want a job. He asks to see my ID and leads me to the bar. Then the bartender tells me to sit and wait for a manager. The manager comes out and immediately pulls up my top to look at my tits. "What size are they?" he asks, just as bored as the cop in the convenience store seemed earlier.

I swallow all my saliva, and my mouth runs dry, but I'm able to choke out, "Thirty-six double D."

"They natural too, sweetie?"

My confidence rises a little. "Yes, sir. Homegrown"

"What's your name?"

My name? Shit. The one thing I can't ever figure out. What's my name? What's a stripper name? Do I give him my stripper name or my real name first? Looking around for anything to call myself, I see a man who looks exactly like Preston emerge from the bathroom. "Preston?" I ask myself, although not quietly enough for Rico Suave not to hear. Now I know my head injury is more serious than I'd thought.

"Preston?" the grease monkey in gold chains yells at me over the music.

Shit. The guy who walked in is Preston. He sees me. Oh, please give me this job. I have to think quickly. "Priscilla. My name is Priscilla. Now do you want these tits out of this shirt on that stage or what?"

He asks for my ID, and I hand it to him seconds before Preston sidles up next to me and places his hand on the small of my back. Ringmaster sees this and firmly says, "Hey, buddy. You gotta pay to play here." Fortunately for me, apparently this stalker just got me a job and made me look super desirable, like I can bring in the money. Boss Man gives me a nod and tells me to get changed in the back. I follow two strippers so I look like I know where I'm going. I have no makeup or stripper clothes, but I have to get my head straight. I have no idea who I am at this point. As I walk toward the back, Preston grabs my hands just as awkwardly as he did yesterday at my normal job when I had a normal life as normal Mary. He asks, "What's your name, young lady?"

I stare at him. His eyes are as deep and dark as ever. I feel his body heat through his hand. Our bodies are somehow getting closer by a seemingly uncontrollable magnetic force, and just as my lips are about to touch his, I snap my hand away and say, "Call me 'Priscilla.'" Then I take off my top and strut to the back without waiting for his response.

I hear him yell after me, "Tease!"

Seducing Mr. Williams

As I enter the back room, I see racks and boxes of clothes, thongs, panties, shoes, wigs, and more. It looks like Barbie's closet threw up in here. Boss Man follows me in, taps my ass, and says, "Wear something pink to match that blond mop up there. We don't have blondes, so you're going to be our little dolly, *capeesh*?" I just nod. He continues, "I assume you know the drill. Get up there, advertise the goods, then push for the close. We sell here—we sell tits, and we sell ass." He looks at my ass and gets a firm grip on both cheeks. "Well, you're lucky you got natural tits and pretty eyes," he says. "Get dressed. Hair Gel out there wants this peanut." He moves hands from my ass to my crotch. "And do something about those wife-beater marks on your head. Keep that shit in your home."

Of course none of the girls are helpful. I watch a few go onstage before me. Most of them don't do anything but dance around the pole and spread their legs to the front row. As I'm about to go up, Preston makes his way to the front. I hear my name being called for me to go onstage, and I freeze. My knees buckle, and I feel like I might throw up. I can't do this; it's all wrong. This isn't me. As much as I desperately want this to be me—as much I want to be Priscilla and make money using my naked body—I can't do it.

I run into the bathroom, and when I finally come out, Boss Man calls me over and tells me I have a thirty-minute VIP with Preston. I don't even know what that means, but Boss Man points to the big rooms to the left. Apparently Preston is more experienced with this than I am, as he leads me to the back. He places the plant in front of the door, and I swallow all the saliva in my mouth, once again running it dry. This isn't going to make for a very good blowjob, if that's what he paid for. How much did he pay? What am I saying? He can afford this. He tips me a hundred dollars for ten-dollar oatmeal and OJ. I don't know anything about him—what he does for a living, if he has a family—and now I'm going to have his penis in my dry mouth. He sits down, and I look at him for a minute then start to kneel in front of him.

"Whoa, whoa, whoa, Mary! Jesus, I didn't know you were that kind of dancer." Mortified, I turn to walk out and run away to anywhere but here when he stops me with his usual grab of my hand. "Will you just sit with me, please?" He's so sweet and caring and looks a little nervous. His brown eyes stare at me, and he smiles. "I guess I should've offered to take you away from all *this*," he says, motioning to the cuts and bruises on my head. "I don't know what you have going on in your life right now," he continues, "but I hope you'll at least allow me to help you, make things a little easier for you."

I start to get defensive. I come from a middle-class family; I have a 4.0 GPA; and I'm really pretty; and here he is thinking that I'm getting abused by my boyfriend and that I'm a cheap prostitute with no sense of worth.

"I don't need your help, buddy, OK? Your help got me fired from my respectable job, remember?"

"What's with the attitude? I'm just trying to help, Mary."

"Fuck. It's 'Priscilla,' for fuck's sake. Can't you get it through your head that I don't want you? I'm not attracted to you. I don't want your money or your hundred-dollar tip so you can jack off to me under your napkin during breakfast!" Yikes. Did I just say that? Oh, fuck you, Gwen for putting that in my head. Shit. I don't want to hurt his feelings; he was just trying to help by giving me big tips.

"I'm sorry. You're right. I'll leave you alone," he says sheepishly, as he starts to walk out.

"Wait, Mr. Williams. I'm sorry. I've had a stressful day. I didn't mean that."

"So you were just teasing me?" he says in a sexual tone.

"What? No. I'm not teasing you. Just…never mind. I never should have told you where I worked."

He walks out, and I sit there, scared about what to do. Should I walk out too? He paid for thirty minutes, and he's walking out after three?

Not more than five minutes later, Boss Man barrels through, moving the plant out of the way. "You, little lady, are fired!"

Part of me is relieved; the other part is insulted. I didn't know it was possible for strippers to get fired. How did I get fired from two jobs in one day? I go to the back room and put away my used panties and pasties. Well, I got to live out my fantasy for one night; this was something new for me. How I yearn to have my boring college life back. I just want to go home, sleep through tomorrow, be back at school on Monday, and grovel to get my job at the restaurant back. Fat Mary knows I make more money for the restaurant than any of the other girls. I'm sure she'll want me back, especially now that Preston won't be coming around again.

As I wait outside for my taxi, I see Preston smoking at the corner by the valet. I walk over to him, still feeling a little guilty about what I said. He's a sweet man and didn't deserve my outburst. "Mr. Williams?" I say in a mouselike voice.

He tosses his cigarette and apologizes. "Nasty habit. Haven't smoked in months."

"Look, I'm really sorry. Today was the worst day you could imagine. You wouldn't believe me if I told you. Then again I don't want to relive it anyway. I just want it to be over, and well, I'm sorry. Will you please accept my apology?"

"No need to apologize. I shouldn't have come. You didn't invite me. It wasn't right of me. I'm twice your age. I should have known better. Heck, I have a daughter who's older than you."

A daughter? Preston has a daughter? Wow. He seems a little more human now. Now I feel really bad. I couldn't imagine my dad being humiliated like I humiliated Preston in there. Then again I couldn't imagine my dad going to a strip club at all.

"I didn't know you had a daughter."

"Two. One's twenty-one, and the other is thirteen. Guess that makes me kind of uncool, huh?"

"No, that sweater makes you kind of uncool," I joke.

"Ah, I'm glad my lack of style amuses you."

"I'm just teasing. You look very handsome as usual." Something in his eyes changes when I say that; his smile fades then reemerges as some sort of menacing grin. I feel his energy change drastically, kind of like the energy I felt in the convenience store earlier. I don't know what it is; I just sense I should be going. "Well, have a good night, Mr. Williams," I say, as I head back to the taxi stand.

"Mary, wait." I turn around at the safe distance I made between us. "Can I at least give you a ride home?"

I think it's a bad idea until I reach into my pocket and realize I spent the last of my cash on that wasted coffee and the cab ride over here. With no other options, I agree.

Preston's car is amazing. I don't know what it's called exactly, but it's red, and the doors go up instead of out. It has a nice tan leather interior, and it's very low to the ground. Our conversation is lacking for the first ten minutes, and then I try to break the tension with a kind gesture. "You really do look handsome tonight, Mr. Williams."

"Why do you insist on calling me 'Mr. Williams'? I've asked you to call me 'Preston.' Am I really that much of an old man to you? I feel like my father when you call me that."

"I'm sorry. I just like calling you that."

"Why?"

"It's sexy." *Oh, Mary,* I think. *What are you doing? You're no longer Priscilla. You're not getting tipped, and you're almost to safety. Why are you flirting? You don't even like sex that much.* Yet somehow I find my hand on his leg; he holds it, and it's so sweet. It's not awkward or forced; it's loving. I feel the love, and I might do him if he weren't my daddy's age.

"Would you like to get some drinks, Mary?" he asks politely.

I want to tell him I want to suck his dick for being my knight in shining armor three times today, but I simply say, "I don't drink" as I move my hand to his inner thigh, feeling him tremble. He's so cute when he gets nervous.

"Mary, are you teasing me?"

"Maybe," I reply with a reassuring smile.

"Would you like to go to my place for a little bit?" he says, his voice quavering. Finally getting the idea, I take off my panties and place them on his rearview mirror, and he speeds off in record time to his home.

His house is beautiful, just like Bruce Wayne's. Who knew Mr. Williams was this rich? Like, I knew he had money…but a mansion? Glass walls, an indoor pool and an outdoor pool—what does he do for a living? I get a little more nervous when he leads me upstairs to the bedroom; I lose my confidence just as quickly as I gained it. He starts to kiss me but senses my nervousness…damn it. We're just kissing, fully clothed. Am I really that rusty? I'm nineteen, and he's old as dirt. Why am I the one who's scared?

"You're not ready for this, are you?" he says, pulling back.

"I just…I don't know. Can we talk first?"

"Why don't I drive you back to your dorm, Mary," he says with disappointment.

I don't necessarily want to go back to my empty dorm room. I don't know what to do, so I think I'll just kiss him. I guess I'm mature enough to handle a make-out session. He's a good kisser, very soft and gentle, and I start to get turned on. His hands run up my legs and under my skirt. Then I feel one finger inside me, then two, pumping me in and out with the same rhythm of his tongue. It feels so good. I'm still pretty tight, so I get a little scared when he puts three fingers inside me. I can tell he's pleasantly surprise by my tightness as his lips turn up in a smile while we passionately kiss.

Preston places my hands on his erection, and I massage it. I'm enjoying myself immensely and don't want him to stop. He goes back and forth between fingering my wet pussy to rubbing my clit oh-so tenderly. I'm so close to orgasm just from his stimulation that I want to make sure he gets the same in return. So I stop him and take off his belt and unzip his pants. I start slowly on the way down, wrap my lips at the bottom of his shaft, and twist my mouth slowly back up. I do this for about forty minutes. I've always enjoyed giving head; to hear a man moan because of me is an amazing feeling. It makes me feel sexy and wanted. When he stops me, I figure he's about to come and doesn't want to finish, so I smile and tell him it's getting late and I probably should get home.

As I start to get myself back together, he stands up. "You're joking, right?" he says in an agitated tone.

"No. I'm tired. I had a long day. This was fun, though. I want to do it again for sure," I reply, as I give him a peck on the lips.

I bend down to grab my purse, and he presses his hands on my shoulders. They feel like fifty-pound weights on either side of me—like sandbags I can't lift up.

"Stay down," he demands. "Finish."

"Preston, I don't want to," I tell him.

He kneels beside me and grabs the front of my throat with one hand. "What did you call me?"

"Preston, please," I plead.

He tightens his grip on my neck. "It's Mr. Williams to you, young lady. Now will you be a good girl and do as I say?"

I nod, trying to catch my breath.

"You want to breathe, little girl?" he says with a smile.

I nod again, and he commands me to get on the bed.

As soon as his hands let go, I bolt for the stairs to run away. It's always a natural instinct for me to run. I almost make it to the front door when his body slams me against it.

"You know you want this. You know you've been teasing me for months for this," he says, as he forces his way inside me from behind.

The coldness of the door makes my nipples erect, and I feel myself get wet inside. I'm getting so much pleasure just by being held here. My body shakes, and tears stream down my cheeks as he glides in and out of me. It hurts so badly; he's so well endowed. It's definitely the biggest cock I've ever felt—and the hardest. I feel it hit parts of me all the way up to my stomach. I feel his throbbing cock in my stomach, and I can't move my body to get in sync with it; he's just having his way with me. He holds it in there for a few minutes at a time, and my body explodes. I drip warm cum all down my thighs and onto his shaft.

"That's a good girl," he says, as he pets my hair. I'm still crying. I'm scared, but my body wants more. "Are you going to continue to be a good girl for me?"

I nod.

He slaps my head and commands, "Say it. Say you'll be a good girl for me."

"I'll be a good girl," I murmur.

"You gonna do as I say?"

"Yes."

"You gonna give me whatever I want, like you said this morning?"

"Yes. Anything you want," I repeat.

Preston pulls himself out of me and throws me to the floor. I cry out as my head hits the cold marble, but he muffles my screams with his hand over my mouth as he enters me once more. "Don't scream, sweet baby," he says. "Just take it."

I don't want it anymore. I'm crying hysterically, begging him to stop. He keeps his hand over my mouth, with the other one stabilizing himself, holding my arm down. I'm so dried up from my orgasm that it really starts to hurt. I feel him tear into my skin. Through his hand, I try to tell him that he's hurting me, and he lifts it to uncover my mouth.

"What did you say, little girl?"

"I said, 'You're hurting me, Mr. Williams.'"

He smacks me across the face. "I'm hurting you? Does this hurt you?" he says, as he strikes the opposite side of my face.

I'm still crying hysterically but try to keep silent. His thrusts quicken as he continues to slap my face, each time harder than the last. He lowers himself on top of me, which forces his erect penis deeper inside me. I close my eyes, waiting for it to end. As he climaxes, he grabs hold of my neck and calls me derogatory names like "whore" and "slut." As I feel him finish, he releases his grip on my neck. When I try to stand up to leave, everything goes black.

3

Taking Control

This past week has been a blur. Haven't washed my hair, and I've barely eaten. I'm surprised I've made it to all my classes. And it's Saturday again; I really hate Saturdays now. I just want to sleep the rest of my life away. I guess that's why people take sleeping pills to off themselves—seems pretty peaceful actually. If my parents call me one more time, I'm downing my whole bottle.

Ring. Ring. Shit. I don't actually want to kill myself. I answer the phone and hear my father and mother. They tell me they're on their way from Van Nuys to visit me since I haven't called them all week. Their idea of visiting me may sound nice, but it's really a punishment; they're checking up on me. Thank God I finished my classes this week. I'm not sure what I'll do if they want to go into the restaurant. Maybe I'll tell them I'm a vegan now.

Surprisingly it's comforting to see my parents. I usually despise their visits and boring chitchat—like they give a fuck about me—but it's nice to feel normal again, or at least as normal as I can feel.

"You look tired, sweetie. Are you getting enough rest?"

"Yes, Mother. All I do is sleep."

"No boyfriends?"

"No, Mother." What's the fucking point of boyfriends? All men are pigs. Then the inevitable is brought up—my job. My father of course has to mention this now; if he only knew the half of it. On the other hand, he probably wouldn't even care. He'd probably say I set myself up to get raped.

"We'll need your half of your tuition so I can send the check in as soon as possible," my dad says.

I gulp. How am I supposed to pay my tuition with no job? All my credit cards are maxed, and I don't even have Gwen or Diesel to borrow money from now. Scenes from the strip club flash in my mind; it's no longer a fantasy but my reality, even though I never actually saw any money from that horrible night. I should've robbed Preston. At least it would have evened the score a little. I mean, after all…wait a minute. He did buy a VIP dance from me, and I never even saw that money. Surely he paid in advance. I didn't even get a tip! Maybe I should go to his house and find something that would be a fair exchange to sell; his place isn't that far from campus. Maybe I could take his car? Sell it for parts? I feel like I've been watching too many episodes of *Breaking Bad*. Why do all the good people in life want to turn bad? But then once you do turn bad, it all goes to crap, which I've learned. This isn't TV; this is real life, and it sucks. Still, fair is fair. Preston took something from me, and I deserve something from him.

"Are you listening to me, young lady?" My father snaps into my thoughts, sending my body into panic mode.

I lose my breath and gasp for air. Beads of sweat roll down my face, and I'm transported back to that night—being shoved up against the wall, getting slapped so hard. My ears start to ring. It's all coming back, even the pleasure I felt. My thighs quiver, and my pussy tingles. Oh, Preston felt so good inside me; he knew what he wanted, and he took it. He was in control. I've never been in control of my life, my diet—nothing. I admire that about Preston. He seized control and took what he wanted, and look at the life he lives because of it. I need to take control. Starting with these fries—fuck these fries. I take the cheese-covered patty out of the bun and eat it with my hands. I need to be a lean, mean fighting machine if I'm going to start taking what's mine. The world owes Mary. Pretty girls like me shouldn't have to fight so hard to make it in this world. I take down my hair, and a new surge of confidence washes over me. A new wind lifts my sails, and it's not an act like Gwen would put on. Oh, no—this is the real deal.

"Yes, Father. I'll get half of it for you this week and the rest of it by the end of the month."

"See? What did I tell you, Frank? She has the money."

Oh, my God. My own father thought I was a deadbeat? He didn't think I'd come through? Why did they visit me—to take me back home with them?

"Your father thought he was going to have a new employee at the grocery store," she continues, smiling.

After lunch with my parents, I go back to my dorm and look through my closet. I toss out all my sweaters and combat boots. Then I find one of Gwen's old sundresses in her dresser and throw it on. It flows over my curves so nicely. My breasts are all but exposed to the nipple, and any sort of wind would lift the skirt and showcase my cheeks. I take off my panties; it feels nice to be completely naked underneath the dress. If Preston wants to have his way with me again, he wouldn't even have to undress me; I'd be ready for him to access. The straps on the dress are so thin that they'd snap if someone wanted to be forceful with me. I glance at my hair in the mirror; it looks so pure. *I* look pure. I was violated just a week ago, yet I manage to look pure. There's a glow—a glow that shows I enjoyed it.

I head out to the campus in my new dress, which showcases my ample body for all to see. I receive whistles and catcalls; a few guys try to be endearing to get my number, but they don't do it for me. The sun is out, and I lay on the grass, daydreaming about Priscilla and Preston. Priscilla would love this dress. Priscilla would love all this attention, and Priscilla would go back to get what was owed to her. Sure, she enjoyed being taken advantage of, but that's her job. Aren't we all supposed to enjoy our jobs? I try to think of which item in Preston's house would be worth the price of rape. He passed out after he unloaded inside me last time; it would be easy enough to take something. I'd just need to focus on the pain so I wouldn't black out again.

I almost can feel Preston release inside me again, when a large body lands on top of me, humping me as if I'm a dog. It's Diesel, with his motley crew looking on, blocking my damn sun. "Get off me, you jerk," I squeak out as he binds my wrists together with one gigantic paw.

"Oh, you know you want this."

I stop fighting him. I stop squirming. I look him dead in the eyes, smile, and whisper, "I do want this but not in front of all your friends." Taken completely off guard, he stands up and looks at his friends then back at me. He mumbles something to his buddies, and they take off, laughing like goons.

I stand up also and brush the nonexistent grass off my ass. "You enjoy my teasing you, don't you?" I ask him coyly. His face lights up with the goofiest grin I've ever seen. "I want you inside me...tonight," I murmur seductively.

"It's Saturday, Mary. I have to go to Gwen's—" He stops midsentence as I adjust my breasts beneath my sheer little gown.

"She doesn't have to know," I say, cutting him off. I put my hands on his belt buckle and look straight up the entire foot between us to show him what it would look like if I went down on him right now. "What do you say?"

"You've always said I disgust you."

"I was just teasing you. It's a game I like to play."

"Game?"

"Yes, I like to pretend I don't want something when I really want it deep down inside. I used to picture you crawling into my bed when

Gwen went to her sorority parties—and you making love to me in the dark. I'd say no, but you know that means yes. I was hoping you'd know that. You didn't?" Diesel shakes his big blond locks, and I feel his jeans tighten from his freshly popped boner. "Shame. I thought you knew I wanted it."

Trying to play it cool, he holds my face in his hands. "I do now. Gwen won't find out?"

"I promise. *No one* will find out."

"What time?"

"Come to my room at ten thirty. Door will be open. I'm going to pretend like you're a jerk and that I don't want you. It'll give me pleasure to have one of my deepest fantasies come true." His lips look like he's about to kiss mine, but I walk away, like the filthy, fucking tease I am.

Back at the dorm, as I get out of the shower, I want to crawl into bed naked, but I really liked the way that sundress made me feel today. It made me feel sweet and girly yet naughty and daring. It reminded me of Priscilla and the night she had with Preston. I really want to go to Preston's tonight; maybe I still can once I finish with lover boy.

At 10:25 it's time to crawl into bed. I feel my juices flowing; I'm already so wet. My pussy throbs, so I tighten my legs, which makes the throbbing even more intense. I've seen Diesel's dick before, and it's done nothing for me, but being in this dress excites me. Being in the dark excites me. Being with Gwen's man excites me. I hear the door creak open just in time. Thank God—I thought I was going to have to resort to putting my phone on vibrate inside me. Diesel hardly makes a sound.

I hear his shoes kick off, followed by his pants unzipping. I hear him put his wallet on Gwen's dresser, like he always did, followed by his phone and keys. He lifts the covers and climbs into bed with me. He spoons me from behind, his full erection in tow.

"Is this what you want?" he asks very sweetly. I ignore him. "Mary, do you still want me?"

"Jesus, Diesel, I told you to just take me."

What a pussy. He's all big and mighty in front of his dumb jock friends, but now that he actually has me, he doesn't know what to do with me. He turns me over to get on top of me. Missionary? This is the only position I've ever seen him in with Gwen. I always thought it looked so boring. I've always found missionary boring—like I just lay there and feel a guy's tip do weird motions.

Diesel does about two pumps, and I feel him already wanting to come. That's when I scream at the top of my lungs, "Help me. Help me. Please, someone, get him off me!"

"What are you doing?" he asks, still inside me but less erect.

"Get off me. I don't want this." I struggle against him as I feel his penis grow back to its erect state, filling me up a little more.

"Oh, your game—I forgot," he says, as he continues to pump away. I try to get up, but he pushes me down, coming inside me then lying on top of me.

"Help me!" I yell. "Someone help me. I'm being raped!"

Diesel cups his hand over my mouth to silence me. "Shut the fuck up!" he barks. "What are you doing? I finished."

He could've fooled me—that's for sure—but I bite his hand and let out a giant yelp. The dorm monitor rushes in with security and a dozen students from my floor. Security rips Diesel off me, and they take him away. The monitor tells me the police are on their way. Out in the hallway, the police arrest Diesel, and I hear him say something about me being crazy and it's all a mistake and his father will be calling them. I rush to my desk to throw Diesel's belongings into my purse, and then I sit on the bed. One of the officers who's questioning me is pretty sexy; I catch him staring at my thighs a few times, which turns me on. I tell him what happened earlier on the campus lawn, which all of Diesel's friends witnessed, as did fifty other people. I tell him how I had to bite him to get him off me just now. My story adds up, and they ask to take me to the hospital so I can get examined and questioned. I tell them I'm too shaken up to go, so the medics examine me in the bathroom.

Just as expected—I got over a thousand dollars in cash, gift cards for gas and coffee, and the keys to Diesel's car. I go down to where his Aston Martin is parked. Seems too hard to sell for parts. Priscilla probably could handle that but not me. Inside the car I find a laptop and an iPad, which I take in exchange for the services I provided. In just a few hours, I already have made more than I made all last semester, and it was something I enjoyed. My father is right; if I find something I love, I'll never have to work a day in my life. I can't believe this was a job—a job I created; a job I started, took, ran with, and now dominate. I'm not worried about Diesel. His father is a lawyer for the college and a ton of public officials, and he'll get his son off with a slap on the wrist. Diesel will probably even get cool points for having done it. Don't all jocks get rewarded for rape these days? That's the way it goes, except I'm in control this time, and it feels good.

When I get back to my room, I'm spent. I don't think I could get wet again if I tried to go see Preston. It sucks that I couldn't finish as well—typical young boys. Preston made sure I had an orgasm. It was good too. Since I'm on a roll, I think maybe I should go see him, but there's always next Saturday.

I toss and turn most of the night. I get up and drink some water, open a window, eat some stale chips, close a window. I wake up at 3:00 am to piss. When I come out of the bathroom, I find Preston sitting on my bed.

4

New Beginnings

I stand there naked, completely shocked and stunned, unable to move. This man I fantasized about hours ago is sitting right in front of me, and I'm terrified.

"You've thought about me, haven't you, young lady?" he says in a very sweet voice. "Come sit by me, won't you, sweet girl?"

Cautiously I walk to the bed; I fantasized about seeing him again, going to his house to take control of my body and my financial situation on my terms. But this isn't on my terms; it's on his, and my body cringes. Here's where real life differs from the movies; you get karma for what you do. This is my payback for pinning rape on an innocent man. Surely the cops coming back a second time for my yelling rape will raise red flags. I suppose this is why they tell you never to cry wolf. The real thing is about to happen, and I don't want it, not like this.

I walk over to sit next to him on the bed, but he stops me. "No. Kneel in front of me," he says. I do as told, looking up at him. "Where's that pretty dress you were wearing in the courtyard earlier today?" he asks.

How long has he been stalking me? It scares me a little to know he saw my every move. Does he know what happened earlier tonight? "Stand up, and go put on that dress for me," he demands in a more seductive tone.

I stand up, walk to the closet, and put on the dress. As soon as it drapes over my body, I feel Priscilla coming out. Priscilla gets excited in this dress; Priscilla wants to be used and abused. My body heats up, and my cheeks blush with anticipation.

He walks over to me and places his hands on my breasts then rests his forehead against mine. He plays with the delicate straps of the dress, and my body quivers. He mumbles something under his breath—something I can't understand—and then he grabs my face and yells, "Do you hear me?" I don't hear anything because my body is too worked up, in hopes he'll have his way with me again. "I know you're not going to tell anyone about what happened last week," he says. "Isn't that right?"

Last week? He's concerned I'm going to tell on him for last week? He did rape me after all, but if he's been stalking me all week, he knows I haven't gone to the police. My heart rate returns to a normal pace, and I'm able to catch my breath again.

"No. I'm not going to say anything."

"That's right. You're not going to say anything, because you wanted it. You wanted it to happen just as much as I wanted it. Isn't that right?" I

38

nod in semi-agreement. He slams my body into the wall and pins me to it with his forearms. "Say yes. Say you wanted it too."

Through tears I tell him, "Yes. I wanted it too."

Preston smacks me across the face and presses his lips against my cheek. "If I see you and the police come within fifty feet of one another again, you, your parents, and their mobile home on Saticoy in Van Nuys will be destroyed. Do you understand me?" I nod, and he moves in to kiss me on the lips. I turn my head every which way to get out of it, but he demands that I kiss him. Finally he gets his kiss and leaves my room.

I've gotten myself in too far. I don't even know what he does for a living. Maybe *this* is what he does. Maybe he makes people disappear. Maybe he's a hit man. I have no idea, but I know I can't go back to his house. It's not a sexual game for him; there's something seriously wrong with his brain. I need to stay normal—get my normal, boring college life back.

The next morning I stop by the restaurant to pick up my final paycheck, praying Fat Mary's not there, but of course, as my luck has been lately, I find her in the back office.

"Well, look what the cat dragged in," she cackles. "Hey, Marty, I thought you said you took the trash out earlier."

She looks better, maybe ten pounds lighter than the last time I saw her, and her hair is a lighter blond, almost the exact shade as mine. She's wearing less makeup too; she easily could pass as my older sister. If it weren't for her atrocious personality and wicked bad accent, she could have any man she wanted.

Tease

"I just came to get my last paycheck," I say as passively as I can to get in and out. Secretly I'm hoping she'll offer me my normal, boring job back, but this is Fat Mary—loud, obnoxious, and insecure—and that's never going to happen.

"Sorry, lady," she says. "I have no idea what you're talking about."

My blood boils. She wants to play games with my money? My hard-earned, much-needed money? "Please, Mary...just give me my money, and you'll never have to deal with me again."

"Aw, what's the matter? Beavers' Damn didn't work out for you?"

I'm mortified. How did she find out? Preston must've told her; that's the only way she could know. "Guess you can't even rely on your looks anymore—can you, Priscilla? I mean, Mary." As my anger rises, I want nothing more than to reach over and beat her to a pulp. But the owner is there, and I can't let him see me crack.

"Fine. Don't give me my money. I'll see you in court."

Fat Mary gives a look to Marty, and he leaves the office. "Oh, look at the big britches on Mary," she says. "The exotic dancer is growin' a pair. You gonna see me in court, huh? How's about I see you in court for all those performance pills I gave ya? You owe me—what?—probably ten grand for all the drugs I provided, you ungrateful little monster. Wonder what the dean would say about that? Lose your scholarship, and your tuition goes up ten times. Yeah, OK. I'll see you in court, missy."

How could she do this to me? I never wanted those pills to begin with. I don't want any ties to her, and she knows that. I can't lose my scholarship; my parents and I can barely afford what we have to pay now. I can't quit school and become a stripper—that was always my plan B, but what do you do when your plan B has failed before plan A?

I'm fuming but can't bring myself to hit her. Heck, I can't even bring myself to cuss her out. So I just walk away silently. That seems to be me, Silent Mary. No-Backbone Mary, as the kids in high school used to call me. I'm so tired of not being able to stand up for myself. Why couldn't Priscilla have helped me with this one?

Sitting on the street corner again, I reach into my bag and find Diesel's wallet. Last night feels like such a blur, like it wasn't real. I feel as if everything that's happened these past couple weeks hasn't been real, like some bad dream I can't wake up from, like one of my fantasies minus the reality.

I go to a convenience store to wire money to my parents. Not more than a few minutes after the transfer is made, my father calls me to tell me how proud he is of me for coming through. Yeah, I framed an innocent boy for rape, robbed him, and enjoyed the whole process; I'm a real trophy daughter. I'll admit, though, that it does feel good to hear the word "proud" in the same sentence as my name coming from my father.

My mind wanders back to Preston, but why? Why do I still desire him? He scares the shit out of me, and he's mean and he's forward…he's basically my dad. Shit. Do I want to fuck my dad? No. Preston's not my dad—he's *like* my dad; there's a difference. Still Preston always wanted to take me out, and he always respected me before. I gave it up too easy. No, I told him I was a stripper when I wasn't, which made him lose respect for me, except that wasn't me—that was Priscilla. Maybe he'd still want to take Mary out.

Rummaging through my bag, I find his card. Where did I get this? He never gave it to me. He must've put it in my purse last night, maybe when I was in the bathroom. His card is an eggshell white with black ink, very basic and plain. It just has his name and number with no business or title description. He still respects Mary and desires Priscilla. Perhaps it's all just his game. I'm hip to these new age dominant-submissive relationships; it must be just a game to him. I should've known. That's why I get pleasure from it.

Upon figuring out his game, I decide to call him and let him know I'm ready to play. When I call, it rings and rings, but I get no response. "I'm sorry, but the number you're trying to reach has been disconnected." Disconnected? He just put the card in my purse last night. This isn't my day. It wasn't meant to be. Oh, God, am I bipolar? Now I hate him again? Mary hates Preston now, but Priscilla desires him. Will he come find me? I'm sure he will. I'll just let it rest for now.

A few months have passed since I lost my job, but I've been making more money than ever. A lot of rich daddy's boys go to my school. I don't scream rape anymore; I just take half their cash out of their wallets when they pass out or take a shower. I consider myself a high-end call girl; it's not my fault if they don't realize I'm a hooker. I don't give out free sex—what girl does? I mean, I'm still cheaper than if a guy had to take me out on a few expensive dates; I save them money actually. They get what they want, and I get what I want. Win-win. The sex is so boring, though. I always fake my orgasms, but the boys don't care. I'm lucky if I get drilled for two minutes.

I'm able to support myself fine with my new career, but I had to get a new job at a new diner to mask what I do when my parents come to visit. I like working there anyhow; it provides the normalcy I still crave in my life. I have a few regulars again but no one like table seven—just mundane tippers with mundane lives. I get free food, which is more than I can say about working for Fat Mary. In fact I get so much free food that I'm starting to get an ass, and I like it; it's good for my other business.

With my new "job," I get a lot of frat boys but also a few professors who rarely carry cash on them. I do that more for the thrill. I set up a little spy cam in my room so I can record it all. I like to watch all the men who come in and use my body. It gets me off a little, but it's nothing like what I had with Preston. I often fantasize about him, more so than I've fantasized about anything else. I guess he didn't realize I found out about the game and was OK with it, but maybe the thrill is gone anyhow now that I know it was role-playing of sorts. My sex life probably never will be the same, but sex always has been lacking for me anyway, so what's the difference? It's better to have been fucked good once than never to have had an orgasm at all.

Tonight is the night of my twentieth birthday, and I have to work. I'm fine with it; I haven't spoken to Gwen since our blowup in the common area, but that's life. I'm thriving now; I'm wearing a little more makeup, and I've bought a few new strappy, flowy, baby-doll dresses—my new favorite thing to wear. Gwen would be so jealous that she wouldn't be able handle our friendship now anyway.

The dinner shift has ended, and things start to slow down when I hallucinate. I see Preston and Fat Mary. This isn't real. I blink twice, shake my head, and see them opening the front door, walking in together. Fat Mary has lost even more weight than I she had a few months ago, Preston looks a little worse for the wear, but he still arouses me. Why are they here? My heart feels like it's about to jump out of my chest. I try to hide, but it's too late. Fat Mary spots me and makes a beeline to my counter. I'm the only one bartending and serving, and I panic. Fat Mary is all smiles as she heads toward me—to show off, I suppose, or perhaps she's going to mock me. As soon as Preston makes eye contact with me, his smile fades, and I feel his nervous energy once again, just like the old table seven I remember. Mary sits herself down and pulls Preston next to her; she drapes herself around him, already a little intoxicated. "Well, look at this sexy little thing. How've you been? Mary, Mary, quite contrary, how does your garden grow?"

"Hi. Can I get you something to drink? Menus?" I say, trying to be as professional as humanly possible.

"Oh, Mary, lighten up. Will you, honey? Come give me some sugar," she slurs as she reaches across the counter to give me a kiss, which might as well have been on my lips. Preston is getting more uncomfortable by the moment, so I try to break the ice.

"Hello, table seven. It's been a while. How have you been?"

"Fine. Thank you," he says without making eye contact. As he motions to Fat Mary for them to leave, beads of sweat run down his face. What's the big deal? Clearly I haven't turned him in for a few months now—what does he have to be nervous about? And I don't plan to make a scene here. It doesn't make sense. Fat Mary continues to be a drunken mess but demands they eat right there because she's hungry.

I serve them, and it's as awkward as you'd imagine it would be. The whole time Fat Mary is hitting on me more than she is Preston. I look at Fat Mary, though, and she's no longer really fat; she looks great actually. I guess if she's dating now, she has a reason to keep the weight off. I wonder if she's actually happier too. She was such a nightmare to work with, and she still owes me money, but I suppose I shouldn't get greedy now that I have two sources of income.

It's almost closing time when they leave. I still have to close the bar, which means I have at least two more hours ahead of me. Preston is so damn cute. I wanted so badly for him to take me right on the bar. I bet the sex would have been amazing. How is someone who's blessed with such a huge penis and huge bank account so kinky? You can't find that shit every day. I can't believe how attracted I still am to him; it's like a magnetism. I guess I should've taken him up on his date offer before I introduced him to Priscilla. Priscilla is what killed it for me, I think.

Seeing Mary and Preston on their date kind of made me long for that—to be carried back home to my bed by a charming gentleman. Fuck. They're probably going to have amazing sex tonight. I wonder if he's going to take advantage of her. Maybe I would've enjoyed my night with him better if I were drunk first. Thanks again to my wonderful parents for denying me the opportunity to ever get drunk. I refuse to turn into them. My parents are crazy, but I'm not. I can't go down their misguided path. Since I come from a family of drunks, you might think I'm mental too, but I'm not. Thank the Lord for that one. Just because your parents are fucked up doesn't mean you will be.

As I'm closing out, my manager asks if I need a ride home. I decline because I want to walk for a while and clear my mind of tonight's events. I brought one of my old sweaters, and I can't wait to cuddle up in it and walk home to enjoy what's left of my birthday. Wait—I'm a hot, single twenty-year-old on her birthday night, and all I can think about is wrapping myself up in an old sweater? This is how I know I'm still normal. Well, I guess that's not really normal; it's boring. But it's nice to have my boring life every now and again.

I take my tips and lock the front door, and then I hear a noise coming from the back room. "Scotty?" I call out cautiously as I pick up a butter knife. Fuck. I'm walking toward the noise; I've yelled out to see who's there; and now I'm taking a butter knife to defend myself against who knows what. This is how all the horror movies play out, and it never ends well for the victim. So I do what they never do—I unlock the front door and bolt outside to call the police. As soon as the door unlocks, I don't get more than a foot outside when a dark, cloaked stranger grabs me and covers my mouth with his hand.

Something's Going Down

I know this scent, and I know this hand. This isn't a stranger. This is Preston. My heart leaps with excitement. Is he going to take me around the corner and have his way with me? So...he left Fat Mary for Sexy Mary. He feels my body loosen up and releases his hand from my mouth. He takes a few steps back so that we're a safe distance apart. Why is he standing so far away from me?

"Are you OK?" he asks with complete sincerity.

"Aside from almost getting kidnapped just now, I think I'm OK," I joke, but he isn't amused.

"What's going on in there?"

"I heard a noise in the back."

"Let me take you home," he offers, in the kindest voice I've ever heard from him. It's also the softest I've ever heard him speak, even before he met Priscilla.

"No. That's OK. I have to go close up."

"I'm going back in there with you," he demands.

"I'm fine, really. You're not allowed in there after hours anyway. If my boss found out, I'd be out of another job because of you. You wouldn't want that on your conscience, would you?"

Still standing at an unusually far distance from me, he caresses my hair and face. He's being so sweet and tender, which makes me lose my attraction to him by the second. I want to get back inside, close up, and leave. This night has been really weird, and I just want my sweater and my nighttime walk alone. After an awkward minute of him feeling my flesh with closed eyes, he hands me some money for a cab so I won't have to walk home so late—two hundred dollars to be exact. Two hundred dollars for a five-minute cab ride seems a bit excessive, but after all, he still owes me for his night with Priscilla in the VIP room.

I take it, and he leaves coldly—no hug, no kiss, no exchange of phone numbers. Doesn't he want to see me again? Why didn't he give me his information? He knows everything about me, but I know nothing about him except his home address, which I guess is really everything someone needs to know if you really think about it. I dated a guy earlier in the summer who never invited me to his place, and it was the weirdest thing. I was good enough to hold his penis inside me but not good enough to see where he lived. I start to turn around to finish closing when I see Fat Mary stumble toward the door.

"You little whore." She's slurring so much that it sounds like a different language.

"Mary—oh, goodness. Where did you come from? Didn't Mr. Williams take you home earlier?"

Propping herself against the door, she says, "I know all about the money. The men. I know everything." How could she have possibly found out about my other life? There's no way she found out. Although she does know Diesel's father, who often comes into the restaurant where she works. Did he say something to her? He must've found out about the missing wallet. As I try to help Mary stand up, she continues to slander me. "I know what you are. I know what you've done. And I'm going to tell. You're done, Mary. Done."

My heart races, and my body goes numb. Am I having a heart attack? I drop my attempt to prop her up and fall to the ground myself, landing right on my bum. Then I start to cry.

"The little whore is crying 'cause the little whore got found out," Mary mocks me. "Taking money for your little pussy—you should be embarrassed. Everyone is going to find out tomorrow. Everyone."

The tears stop streaming, and my heart calms its pace. I look up at Mary, who's stumbling, trying to keep her balance, and I see the light-blue toilet paper from our bathroom hanging out of her jacket. It must have been her who was in the back of the restaurant. Would she have confronted me inside if I had stayed in there? She's probably going to try to make me turn myself in. I stand up, grab her by her now bony elbow, drag her back inside the restaurant, and lock the door.

"What the hell are you doing? Let go of me," Mary demands, as if she has any control over the situation.

"Oh, Mary, you're drunk," I tell her. "I'm going to take you home."

"I don't need your help, you whore…you dirty, filthy whore. Go fuck men for money, you worthless cunt."

When she says that word, I look at her mouth. It's covered in smeared lipstick, but her gloss is still intact, which makes her lips look juicy. I have to taste them, and they're just as soft as they look. She keeps fighting back and calling me names; I have to shove a napkin in her mouth to keep her quiet. I wonder if her lips in her panties taste as good. I immediately go down on her—no foreplay. She's very dry, so I moisten her up with my saliva. I can tell she prepared herself to get fucked tonight—freshly shaven, smells like baby powder; mmm…delicious. I feel her struggle, which makes me enjoy it even more.

I'm getting some of her juices in my mouth when I feel a knee to my nose. Bitch. She runs in a zigzag motion to the back of the restaurant. I only have to walk at a slightly faster pace than usual to keep up with her. As soon as she gets to the door, I slam her head against it, and she falls to the floor. I wait for her to regain consciousness so she can enjoy what I'm going to do to her next.

Mary finally wakes up on top of the counter, where she was flirting with me earlier in the night. I have her tied down to it with some zip ties. She's crying as I have a firmer gag in her mouth this time so she can't spit it out. Straddling her, I say, "You little tease, you—coming in here, making me all jealous with Preston then kissing me. I know you want this." I hear her plead for mercy, mumbling "Mary" through her gag. "Mary isn't here. She went home for her birthday. My name is Priscilla."

I pick up the butter knife and wet it with my tongue. I insert it inside her and hear her shriek with delight. Woman must've never been fucked with a dildo before. I continue as her body goes out of control. I can't see her face, but I know I'm giving her the best death she could've asked for. I pick up a fork to give her a more intense sensation. In and out—I feel my own excitement rise. As more blood comes out, her body stops fighting. Bitch isn't going to ruin my future for the second time. Why do formerly fat, gross girls turn into such raging bitches after they become pretty? Plus she's drunk—like, how much more pathetic can you get? I have no room in my life for drunks, and this drunk messed with the wrong cunt. Fuck, I didn't even get off. She had to go and ruin it with her knee to my perfect nose.

Surprisingly my nose is fine; there's just a little cut on it. I look at the blood near the back door and the blood on the counter and realize I have a long night ahead of me.

6

Role Playing House

I wake up to someone pounding on my door. It's the police. I scrounge to find a sweater for my naked body and come up with a hoodie that belongs to some kid who fucked me last week. I open the door and see two strapping policemen. Still foggy from waking up, I invite them in. The questioning begins about some murder that took place last night at the diner. I have no idea what they're talking about. I answer all their questions and give them my complete cooperation, but they still insist on bringing me to the station.

At the station I barely can sit up—like I have what I imagine a hangover to be like. I can hardly see, or make out any of their words. They keep asking me where I was last night; I tell them I don't remember because I don't. They try the good cop/bad cop routine, but I have nothing to hide. Perhaps I should've gotten a lawyer. Ah, who am I kidding?

I can't afford a lawyer. They leave me alone in the room for what feels like hours, and eventually I fall asleep. Awakening me for a second time today, they tell me I'm free to go because my alibi arrived. When I walk out of the interrogation room, Preston is standing there, waiting for me. He thanks the police, and the chief gives him a hug. Huh? I can't comprehend any of it, but I'm starving, and Preston looks amazing, so when he offers me breakfast, how can I refuse?

We get into a car that I don't recognize as being his. As we're driving to go get food, he seems very polite and sweet, like the father I've always wanted.

"What did you tell them?" I ask, trying not to sound too accusing.

"You were with me last night."

"I was?"

"Yes."

"I didn't do it," I tell him.

He looks at me and smiles—a smile like he doesn't believe me.

"I couldn't kill anyone. That's not me."

He changes the subject. "Mary, do you realize this will be our first official date?"

"You don't even really like me, Mr. Williams. I don't even have your phone number."

"Do you need it?"

"Well, no," I say. "I guess not."

"Would you like to get to know me, Mary? I'd like to get to know you."

"Why?" I hiss.

"Because I think we're a lot alike, you and I."

I chuckle mockingly. There's no way in hell we're anything alike. We can't be more different, but I'm so excited to be taken out for once. As much as I love the money I get in exchange for my body, I'd like to be treated like a lady more often.

At the restaurant I can't really eat anything. My body is still in shock from my hearing about Fat Mary's death. What could have happened? I don't understand. Who would want to kill her? She was loud, but she also was just an average chick who really wasn't going anywhere in life much beyond management at a shitty little restaurant.

When the check comes, I reach into my bag to pay for my half of the meal. I take out my wallet, which has more than five hundred dollars in it, mostly singles. This doesn't make sense. I never make more than a hundred in tips at the new diner. How did I get all this money? Preston couldn't have put it in there so quickly. Are the police trying to set me up? Is Gwen trying to frame me for something? She does still have a key to my dorm room. I wonder if Fat Mary told anyone about my hooking. I wonder if Preston knows.

Preston insists I put my money away, and I do so without hesitation. I don't want anyone to see how much money I have. I'm becoming more paranoid by the minute. I don't want to hook anymore. My tuition is covered for a while, and I'll just step up my hours at work. Hooking wasn't worth it, but breakfast with Preston is. Maybe I could have a nice, normal, healthy relationship and a nice, normal job while I continue my nice, normal education.

Preston and I go to his house, and it's so different than I remembered it being. It's still huge, but this time around, it has a light. There's a warmth when I walk in, which makes my heart happy. He shows me some designs of model homes; maybe he's an architect. I swim in his pool while he watches; he says I remind him a lot of his daughters. He has a daughter around my age and another in middle school. It's nice to see the human side of him. I try to skip over my family history, but he insists.

I get out of the pool, and he covers me in layers of towels. I find it odd 'cause he isn't the least bit interested in my body today. I don't understand it.

We have lunch inside then talk for a while. Things turn serious real quick.

"Have you told anyone about us?" he asks matter-of-factly.

"No. I mean, what's there to tell?"

"If you go to the police, everything you have and everything you know will be gone. I got you out of trouble today, but I can and will get you into a whole lot worse if you cross me, Mary."

I'm terrified and want to leave, but then I remember what happened the last time I got up to leave without his consent.

"I won't say anything," I tell him. "I had fun. We were just messing around, right?"

"Is that what you think? Are you a whore, Mary?"

"You know what? Fuck you!" I say, getting up to go. I expect him to come up and grab me or chase me down, but he doesn't.

I make it halfway down the driveway when he comes out and yells at me to wait up. "I'm sorry," he says. "I really am. I know what you've gotten yourself into. But if you'll let me, I want to help you." I look at his soft-brown eyes and feel his sincerity. He scares me and confuses me, but he also makes me feel safe. He continues, "You think I came in every day for that terrible oatmeal? I came in for you."

"You know nothing about me," I say flatly.

"I know more than you think."

How has he transformed from the sweetest guy into the creepiest in a matter of minutes?

"I want to protect you. I want to take you away from everything, Mary," he says, as he brushes my hair behind my ear. He holds me in his driveway in the warmest embrace I've ever felt. My parents never give me hugs. I don't even remember the last time someone hugged me. It feels so good; it's something I've longed for without even knowing it. Tears stream down my face, and I can't control them. "What is it, sweet girl?" he asks, holding my face and staring at me with his deep eyes.

So many emotions pour out of me. I don't know what I'm feeling, perhaps a bit of regret, a little contentment, some sexual tension…I love him. I can't believe it because I've never been in love before, but I'm in love with Preston Williams. How can I be in love with someone I barely know? He kisses my lips so gently that it sends shivers down my body. I start to tingle. After kissing my lips, he moves down my neck. He pulls down the straps of my dress to expose my breasts and kisses them tenderly. The warmth of the sun reflecting off the pavement makes my whole body shake. He wraps his lips around my nipples while firmly holding my breasts. I run my fingers through his unkempt hair and moan. Then his hands find their way up my skirt and under my panties.

He kneels and focuses on taking off my panties. His tongue enters me, and my knees quiver so much that I might fall back in euphoria. I really can't take the teasing; I need him inside me, but when I motion for him to stop so he can take me completely, he shakes my hips firmly to let me know he's going to stop when he wants to, and there's nothing I can do about it.

Cars drive by. I'm not sure what they can see, but I love it. I love that he doesn't care, that he wants to take care of me. As the cars rush past and his tongue goes deeper and quicker, my whole body tenses. I'm holding my breath, trying not to make a mess all over him; I almost get a headache. I try my best to resist releasing. He hasn't even gotten his dick wet, and I'm about to finish. I don't want to be selfish, but then he commands me to come. He says he wanted to taste my juices. He says it would turn him on; it would make him happy. My body can't hold back any longer, and I drench his mouth with all my secretions. He comes up to kiss me, and I look at him, slightly embarrassed from the amount that came out of me. He kisses me and tells me to taste what I taste like. I return the favor by going down on him and slowly sucking his erect penis for everyone to see. He gets so turned on so quickly, like one of my regular boys from the dorms. It's like he's nineteen again and can't contain his excitement. He pushes me down to stop so he won't ejaculate too fast, and without taking off my dress, he enters me right on the driveway. He holds me tightly and kisses me while making love to me. I tell him, "I love you," and he busts right inside me and immediately stands up.

"What's wrong?" I ask, confused as to why suddenly he doesn't want to be close to me.

"What you said—why did you say that?"

"What did I say?" I ask coyly, trying to pretend I didn't say it out loud.

"You know what you said. Did you mean it?"

"Yes, Preston, I did."

"You called me 'Preston.'"

"Is that OK?"

"If you tell me you love me, and then I find out you didn't mean it, I'll fucking lose it. I'll fucking lose my mind if I find out you're just fucking with me."

Seeing that he's scared and also emotionally attached to me, I awkwardly grab his hands the way he grabbed mine at the restaurant months ago. "Preston, I love you. I think about you constantly. I think about making love to you, but I also think about your eyes and your soul and everything you've done to get me. And now I'm madly in love with you. So yes, I love you."

"I love you so much, sweet baby," he says. He kisses me for a minute then embraces me for what seems like forever; I wish it would last forever.

Preston and I make love a dozen times that afternoon. It's so beautiful. Then we go out to dinner and come back to his place and make love again and again. It's all very sweet and romantic. Around 2:00 a.m., I realize I have class in six hours and have to leave. When I start to get my clothes on, Preston becomes very agitated.

"Where are you going?"

"I have to get back to my place and get some sleep."

"Stay," he says. "I'll drive you back in the morning."

"Preston, it's morning, and we both know I won't get any sleep if I stay," I tell him with a wink and a smile.

"You said you loved me. You said you'd let me take care of you."

"I do, and I will. But I have school and work and a million other things I've got to take care of this week."

"You're going to go fuck those boys, aren't you? Which one is it going to be tonight? Aston Martin? Porsche? Range Rover?"

"Have you been spying on me?" I ask, terrified by what he knows about me.

"I know all about you, Mary. If you leave, you'll regret it"

"You don't scare me anymore, Preston." I barely get that out before he comes up to me and shakes me by the arms.

"You'd better start getting scared."

"You're hurting me," I say, trying to free myself from his grasp, but he pushes me to the floor.

"Get up. Get up and walk out right now. I dare you."

"You're insane…you know that? You're crazy. I'm crazy for ever coming here." I run out of the bedroom and bolt down the stairs, my heart racing. I'm sure he's going to follow me, but he doesn't.

I dash outside to the street and hitch a ride back to the dorms.

I'm so confused. Preston really has been stalking me. He knows more than I thought he did. I can't continue to see him; that wouldn't be fair to either of us. I need to focus on school and work again. If I stop hooking right now, I'll be fine. I'm not in too deep yet.

I can't sleep, knowing he knows my every move. I don't know what to do. I'm sure he'll be back or find a way to run into me.

In class the next morning, the cops come into my English lit class and tell me I'm under arrest for the murder of Mary McEnroe. I didn't kill her; someone must have framed me. I look at Gwen's face, and she's pale as a ghost. She tells me she'll call Diesel's father to help.

As I sit in jail, they tell me they have enough evidence to convict me. I'm appointed a lawyer, who suggests I take a plea bargain. Gwen is my first visitor. She arrives and hugs me and apologizes for everything. She tells me she's missed me, and I tell her I've missed her. She's my best friend and always has talked sense into me. She says Mr. Bloom, Diesel's father, will come down to represent me. I tell her I didn't kill Mary, and she believes me. "No one's going to buy that little ol' you could kill someone," she says. "It's just not going to stick, Mary. You'll be OK."

I sit in jail for two days. Gwen doesn't show up again, and neither does Diesel or his father. I've missed two whole days of classes and work, and now I'm facing serious prison time. I'm told I have a new lawyer and will get to meet with him the following day.

The whole night I look around me and realize this could be my life for the next however many years. I try to stretch my brain back to that Saturday night. I remember seeing Preston and Mary at the bar, and I remember talking to Preston outside after closing, but I don't remember anything after that. There is the possibility that I did go home with Preston. Perhaps that was why he felt compelled to help me by providing an alibi. But how in the world did I end up in jail?

When I go to meet my lawyer, a part of me feels safe and another part is scared shitless. You'd think it would be a surprise, but it wasn't—Preston is my new court-appointed attorney.

"Oh, God. Please tell me you're not here for me."

"Mary, I told you what would happen if you crossed me. I can make all this all go away for you right here, right now, if you'll just let me take care of you." I stare at him in disbelief. I didn't know whether I should trust him, but what choice do I have? "Do I frighten you, Mary?" I nod, and he lowers his head in shame. "That's not my intention. I love you and want to take care of you. You don't have to work or go to school. I'll even meet your parents, if you'd like."

"I like school," I choke out, trying to wrap my head around all of this. I'm trying to make sense out of anything at this point.

"I can't have you in a place where I can't control the atmosphere. It's too risky. Look at where you might end up—in places like this." He motions to the cement walls that surround us.

I could spend the rest of my life in prison, or I could spend it with Preston. Either way I'll be a captive. I do love Preston, but he scares me, and I don't want to live my life in fear. My parents would be disappointed if I quit school, but I'm sure they'd die of glee if they saw I was living in Preston's mansion. I wouldn't have to worry about money or problems with the law; he seems well connected in those areas. I look at him sitting there, holding my hands, his eyes pleading me to be with him.

I swallow any doubt and gulp before saying, "You're right. You're always right. I want to be with you."

Preston stands up and hugs my head as I remain seated. "Oh, that's a good girl. I knew you'd come back to me. I love you, little girl. I love you so very much."

Smiling, I say, "I love you too," this time with less certainty than a few days prior.

As promised, I'm released, and Preston's waiting for me. He's driving yet another car I haven't seen before. It's the color of an oil spill—greens and purples—and it glistens in the sun.

"I've taken the rest of the day off," he says. "We're going to get you a new wardrobe."

"What's wrong with the clothes I have now?" I ask, a little offended. I love the baby-doll dresses I've acquired over the past few months.

"Do you like your clothes?"

"Yes. They make me feel girly and pretty."

He smiles. "OK. Then let's get you some food."

Preston spends most of our lunch together on his phone. I keep staring at mine, hoping I'll hear from Gwen, but I don't. Where has she disappeared to? I feel like I'm being ignored, and I hate it. I guess I could play along for a week or so that I'll be Preston's kept woman but no longer than that. After just a couple hours with him, I want to go back into my jail cell, where at least I was free to be me and alone with my thoughts.

When we get to his place, I kick off my shoes and head to the couch.

"No," he demands. "This part of the house isn't yours. Come with me."

I follow him to the basement, which I've never seen before. We have to go through the garage and into another room, which then leads to stairs that are almost fifty steps deep. It feels cold and drippy as we walk what feels like a mile to a beautiful grand door that looks like something straight from the *Titanic*. When I enter, I see a grandiose apartment with huge windows and gorgeous drapes. There's also a gigantic kitchen filled with food and a bedroom with a closet full of bulky sweaters like I used to wear and sheer slip dresses like I've been wearing the past few months. I see all my favorite foods in the fridge and even the exact bath products I have in my dorm. There are fresh lilies in one room, daisies in another, and roses in the bedroom.

"The only thing I don't know about you is your favorite flower. You'll let me know, won't you? I'd like to have fresh ones in here every day for you," he says, clearly a little nervous regarding my reaction to this place.

"Whatever you like," I reply, making my way to the windows. I push back the drapes to see the windows aren't really windows but giant computer screens. There are images of the outside world—dandelions blowing in the countryside in one window and fish swimming in a clear-blue ocean in the next. "What is this place?" I ask.

"It's your new place. I hope you like it."

"I won't be living with you?"

"I can't have people seeing you. You saw the way they looked at us at lunch today and the previous times we've gone out together in public. Plus how will I explain you to my daughters and their mother?"

I'm completely taken aback. Preston Williams is insecure and scared of women and what other people will think of him?

"There will be plenty of food in here at all times for you. If you want any books, I'll get them for you."

"What about my parents?" I ask, suddenly missing the two people I never thought I'd miss.

"We'll have them over to the main house tomorrow, and we'll announce our engagement. I'll set them up with a nice house wherever they want to live and offer to pay for their travel, as they've wanted that for quite some time now—correct?"

How on earth does Preston know that my parents want to travel? I don't want any of this. He wants to hold me down here like I'm an actual captive. He's kidnapping me, and I agreed to it. I can't marry a man who's hiding me away from the entire world.

"You want to marry me?" I ask him.

"Yes. Don't you want to marry me?"

"I won't even be living with you. I'll be living in a shack in your base-ment like a hostage being held against my will."

I immediately regret those words as soon as they come out. Preston raises his hand and gives me a swift smack across the face. It hurts so bad that it feels as though my cheek is bleeding through my pores.

"You wanted this. You told me you love me. You told me I could take care of you."

I whimper like a little baby. My life is completely over, and there's no way of escaping. There's a lock on the outside of the main door, and I realize this is my life; this is what it's going to be. I have to cooperate with him if I want any chance of getting out of here.

"Forgive me, Preston," I tell him.

"Mr. Williams," he corrects me. "From now on you'll refer to me only as 'Mr. Williams,' 'sir,' or 'Master.'"

This definitely isn't a game to him.

"Forgive me, Master," I say, avoiding eye contact with him.

"It's OK, sweet angel." He comes down to my level. "Look at that natural blush in your cheeks. That turns your master on." He pushes me down, onto my back, then turns me around. I hear his pants unzip as he forces himself inside me. He keeps telling me what a "good girl" I am and how he loves me. He grabs my hair so hard that he pulls a chunk of it out. I'm crying hysterically, and he tells me he loves it. He says his baby is serving him what he needs. After he finishes, he stands me up and takes me to the shower, where cleans me off then powders my bum. He even picks out my pajamas. He asks if I want him to come back tonight. I tell him he can do whatever he wants. He smiles and holds me until I fall asleep.

When I wake up the next day, I find a new baby-doll dress hanging in the living room of my basement apartment. It's a rust color and a lot longer than the ones I've been wearing lately. I explore my new living quarters. The place is beautiful, but I feel so alone. I mean, I'm used to being alone in my dorm and keeping to myself in general, but it was nice to get out among people, even if there was no interaction. In the kitchen I find more food than I ever could consume; surely it'll go bad before I can eat it. Wait—maybe he's trying to fatten me up. Oh, no, what if he's a cannibal? What if he wants to sell me off to other cannibals? Maybe that's his business. I decide against eating anything.

I hop in the shower then dry myself off and put on my new baby-doll dress. It's really pretty. I pretend that I'm a princess who's locked away in a tower and that my real Prince Charming is going to save me. Hopefully it'll be a prince from the Middle East so Preston never can track me down, and if he does, he'll be decapitated. I throw my hair into a topknot and decide to go back to bed. I have no idea what to do with myself.

I'm woken up by Preston cuddling me. "You're skin is so soft," he whispers as he gropes my leg.

"You startled me."

"I didn't mean to frighten you, my baby. Did you sleep well? You smell impeccable."

"Yes. Thank you. All I do is sleep."

"Lets get you to the salon to get your hair done," he continues.

"My hair done for what?"

"Our engagement announcement to your parents and Gwen."

"Engagement?" I look down at my hand; apparently he slipped the ring on my finger while I was sleeping. I don't even get a proposal? "Why do you want to marry me? You already have me here forever."

"It wouldn't be right for us to continue our sexual relations unless it's right in the eyes of God and the State of California," he says in a completely serious tone.

It wouldn't be right for him to rape me without God knowing he was committed to me? This makes no sense. His own children don't even know I exist. Will they come over to play, not knowing Daddy is keeping another child downstairs? Is Preston going to want more kids with me? I've heard of this stuff on the news; the kidnappers impregnate their hostages, and their victims start believing they have a normal life.

I have to plan my escape. I have get to my parents before Preston gets to them. We have to move; I have no money, but it doesn't matter. I'd live under a bridge at this point. He continues to hold me and stroke my hair; he sniffs my skin and tells me how much he loves me. I tell him I love him too just so he'll believe I want to be there as much as he thinks I do. He makes tender love to me, and I hate to say it, but I enjoy it. He does know how to fuck a woman. In the moments of our lovemaking, I'm not scared; in fact I'm content.

After we go to the salon, he takes me to lunch and tells me to eat heartily, as we'll no longer be dining in public.

When we get home, I wait next to the door to the garage to be taken down to my quarters.

"What are you doing?" he asks.

"Waiting to go back to my living area. Aren't you going to take me down there, Mr. Williams?"

"Please, it's 'Preston.' Call me 'Preston,' silly girl. And of course not. Let's go for a swim before we start dinner for our guests."

Preston or Mr. Williams? Which fucking one is it? This guy is going to drive me insane before I can escape. I might as well start installing padding in my quarantine.

We swim and talk like we did when I knew him as table seven. He's very endearing and normal. You'd think we were a typical couple. It's nice to be in the fresh air, but I'm worried how dinner will go. Surely Gwen will catch on that something isn't right, and she'll find a way to get me out of this mess. I'm sure my mom and dad will probe me about why I quit school. How will Preston get me out of that one?

Without any briefing, we start dinner, and my parents arrive with Gwen in tow. Apparently Preston doesn't have any worries about their approval of our relationship. Boy, is he in for a rude awakening.

7

Coqueta

The beginning of dinner is extremely awkward. My father keeps asking Preston and me about how we met, and my mother keeps questioning why I never spoke of Preston before. Gwen rolls her eyes at everything Preston says. It's all extremely uncomfortable, especially for Preston. He becomes increasingly agitated with each new question about his past, my past, and our past together.

He cuts dinner short and asks me to help him get dessert ready in the kitchen. As soon as we get there, he grabs my shoulders and shakes me. "What the hell are you doing?" he demands.

"What are you—?"

He covers my mouth to quiet me, and in that moment, my father walks in with my mother and Gwen.

"That's it. We're leaving. Mary, you're coming with us," my father grumbles.

Preston immediately lets go of me and tries to reason with my parents, saying it isn't what it looked like. Then he pleads with me to stay, but I just want to go home. I don't want to play this game anymore. Heck, I don't even want to be an adult anymore; I just want to go home with my parents and crawl into my bed.

My father threatens Preston and tells him never to come near me again. Preston looks as his life has been taken from him. His eyes appear lifeless, and he's on the verge of tears. I leave without anything; my parents tell me I don't need anything from his house, which is fortunate, because I have no idea how I would explain my living quarters to them. We ride in silence all the way home.

The next morning I wake up to a new smartphone next to my bed. It has only one number in it—Preston's. I don't use it or touch it. My parents are letting me get a job instead of going back to school; they ask if I want to move, and I tell them I no.

I don't want to go back into food service, so I start as a receptionist at a shipping warehouse. For the most part it's nice to be secluded and working alone, but after a few weeks, I find myself picking up the phone, wanting to call Preston. Why do I miss him so much? I know it's better for me not to call him; I've got to find something to occupy my time.

I start to date the boss's son, Brad. He's in med school and gorgeous and all-American. My parents love him; his parents love me; and we date for six months before having sex. When we finally do have sex, it's vanilla. He gets on top of me, pumps it, then shoots inside the condom. Then he takes off the condom off and goes to sleep. It isn't anything magical—how much magic can happen in six minutes?

I find myself getting bored again—bored of Brad, my parents, my job, my life. And I find myself thinking not only of Preston but also Priscilla. I'm Priscilla, not Mary. Mary's going to get knocked up then be bored the rest of her life, but Priscilla isn't going down that road.

At night I go out to bars, flirt with guys, and go home with them. It's fun and exciting. The ones who don't wear condoms are always the most fun; it's like playing Russian roulette. They're living dangerously, as am I. Soon afterward, though, I start to get bored with it. What happened to me? I use to be a sex goddess; now I'm just a random lay with random Joes.

Deciding sex isn't doing it for me, I start to flirt with married men while their wives are nearby. I love to catch them in the bathroom while their wives are at the table. I tell them I've been watching them and will do anything to have their dick in my tight pussy. Every time I can see their eyes bulge out of their pants, if you catch my drift. They're so perverted; it's disgusting. I always see who will take the bait then tell them to call me.

Carl is my first catch; he likes what I'm selling. He's a former racecar driver whose wife was hot forty pounds ago. We bang in my bed, which

I've been sharing with Brad ever since I moved in him a few weeks ago. When Brad comes in and finds us, he threatens to leave me, but like the little puppy he is, he comes crawling back the next day, begging me to stay. He asks me to stop seeing Carl, but I say no. He says, "Fine but not in our house." That's OK—I start doing Carl in Brad's father's office. It's exciting.

Brad and I get more serious. On both Christmas and New Year's, he asks me to marry him, but I decline. Then Valentine's Day rolls around, and he asks me again. This time I say yes. It's a funny thing—Brad puts up with my sexual perversions, and I like that. He doesn't understand, but he's my submissive, and I need that. It's refreshing, and it's nice to know he loves me unconditionally.

Carl tells me he's leaving his wife; I tell him not to and that I'm engaged now. He doesn't understand, and I love it. I've told him I love him but never meant it. I've told all the guys from the bars that I love them. Many left their wives for me, but I was doing their wives a favor by leading the stray dogs away. I kind of feel like a missionary, doing some sort of divine intervention.

After a fuck session behind a liquor mart, Carl asks to take me out. I don't like the idea, but it's getting dark. I tell him I'll pick the place. I take him to the Car Wash, a high-end strip club near the airport. He seems confused, but I tell him not to question me. We watch the girls dance, and I can tell he's turned on. I tell him to call me "Priscilla" and meet me in the last handicapped stall in the men's bathroom in five minutes.

I get completely undressed then hear a very low voice say, "May I come in?"

Seductively I ask, "What's my name?"

The voice replies, "Priscilla," and I tell him it's open.

I'm already on my stomach, with my ass in the air, and I tell him to put his dick wherever he wants. I tell him how badly I crave his cum inside me. He holds my hips tightly against his pelvis. Then he rocks deeply back and forth and thrusts so hard that I hit my head on the toilet. He keeps thrusting into me, and I keep hitting my head. I ask him to stop as he thrusts into me and pulls out, knocking my head straight onto the ceramic tile.

"What the fuck?" I say, barely conscious.

I turn around and see Preston. He puts his hand on my mouth, just as he did last year in his kitchen, and tells me to shut up.

He tells me I'm going to walk out of there with him, and if I don't, he's going to cause trouble. I tell him I'm not scared of him, and truthfully I no longer am. The way Preston cowered when my father took me away wasn't a turn-on.

His eyes fill with worry at the thought of losing me again.

"Why don't you want me?" he questions.

"Preston, I loved you—I *do* love you—but you held me prisoner. That's not a life I want to live."

He asks me why I've been sleeping with so many men that I've picked up at so many bars. "What kind of STDs have you caught?" he snaps at me. I don't know whether to be offended or terrified that he knows so much about my life.

"I don't have anything, asshole," I snap back.

"You didn't love what we just did?" he asks in a sweet tone.

I have to pause; I did love it. I loved it because it was him. When I thought it was Carl, I didn't want it…but when I saw it was Preston, I wanted him to take me and hurt me again and again.

"I loved it, Mr. Williams," I slyly reply, as I take off my panties and put them in his coat pocket. I kiss him on the lips and whisper, "Goodbye, Preston" before slinking past him.

He lets me go, which surprises me. When I go back into the club, it's pitch-black, and there's no sign of Carl. I ask the bartender where he went, and he says he's getting a lap dance. I'm so pissed when I see a naked blonde grinding on Carl's crotch with his disgusting yellow snakeskin boots showing through the bottom of the curtain. I yank him out and ask him, "What the hell?"

"What do you mean?" he says. "You paid for it."

Ugh, I immediately know Preston was involved. I leave Carl there and storm out of the club. As I wait for a taxi, he rushes toward me.

"Let me take you home," Carl insists. I continue to ignore him as I wait for the cab.

Unsurprisingly, Preston comes out of the club at that moment. "Everything OK?" he asks me.

"I'm fine," I retort, not giving either of them the satisfaction they want. I'm the tease, not them. I'm the one who's supposed to be playing a game.

Carl recognizes Preston immediately. "Hey, dude. You were the one who said Mary wanted me to get a lap dance. What the fuck, man?"

Preston looks at Carl then at me. Staring into my eyes, he says, "I have no idea what you're talking about…" Then, looking dead into Carl's eyes and pushing him back a few steps without any force, just smolder, he finishes, "…man."

"Mary, you know this guy?" Carl asks.

"Never met him before," I say, staring at Preston's eyes.

I take Carl by the hand and get him into a taxi. When I tell him I can't wait to have him in the backseat, the tiny vein in Preston's forehead pulsates. I've never felt more turned on, more alive in my life. I have both men drooling over me in my little baby-doll dress.

When we get back to my place, Carl reaches into his back pocket to pay for the taxi but can't find his wallet. He doesn't know what happened, and I tell him I have no money. I make Brad come out and pay for it. When he does, he tells Carl never to come around our house again. I like assertive Brad. He sees my cuts from earlier in the bathroom and brings me inside to care for me as if I'm a wounded little bird.

A couple of weeks have passed, and I haven't heard from Carl. Out of the blue, he sends me an e-mail, saying his wife somehow found out about us. What a pussy. He says she received a call from an anonymous man who saw us at the Car Wash. He tells me we have to be more discreet but says that he's missed me. I write back and tell him we should just stick to my office.

He comes into my office every day at lunchtime, when the white collars are at the steakhouse down the street and the blue collars are at the strip club. I love the blue collars; I've danced for them on the cement poles downstairs for money. It's even earned me the nickname "Coqueta," which is Spanish for "flirt." So sweet—that may even be my new persona. Forget Priscilla; that murderous mess is no longer me. Coqueta is who I am. Coqueta has fun, and no one gets hurt.

I ask Carl to call me "Coqueta," and he does. I tell him I'm going to call him "Preston." It's so hot—banging on the plants, the bench where clients wait, even in the kitchen where everyone eats. He doesn't have Preston's passion, but when I close my eyes, I snap a rubber band on my wrist to feel a little pain while Carl drills me from the back. Aside from Preston, he's the only one who can properly dig me out from behind. He couldn't get as deep as Preston, though. When Preston had his belt around my neck, he'd pull me into him so deeply that I thought my organs would erupt. It felt amazing; his cum filled my stomach and warmed my whole body, and what was left over would drip down my thigh. Carl can't even finish all the time. He says it's age; then he says it's performance anxiety. Then it's drinking and then nervousness...excuse after excuse.

One day we're fooling around on my desk in broad daylight, where anyone can walk in, and on that rainy afternoon in April, someone does—Carl's wife.

Six gunshots are fired, and our bodies fall to the floor.

8

I come to in a hospital bed. At first I don't know if I'm in heaven or hell or some sort of limbo, but it just ends up being a bed in the pediatric ward for some reason. I see a bunch of cops in the hallway and am terrified. I've gotten out of a few sticky situations with the law; I don't want to press my luck. I want to call my parents or Brad but don't even a chance before the nurse walks in.

"Good, you're awake, Mrs. Williams," she chirps. Huh? How long was I out of it for? Is this a dream? A bad trip? I don't even know my own name. "Your husband went to sign you out and bring you a jacket. He should be back any minute."

I glance down at my hand and see my engagement ring from Brad. This has to be a bad dream, but nope, in walks Preston, beaming from ear to ear. I ask where Carl is, where Brad is, and whether my parents know where I am.

The nurse asks, "Who's Brad?"

Preston replies, "She hasn't heard anything yet. She's still a little out of it. Could you get us a wheelchair so we can leave?"

"Preston, where's Carl?" I demand.

"Carl was shot," he says, "by his wife. Apparently he was cheating on her, and she caught them in their bed."

No. That's not the case. I know Carl wasn't seeing anyone else. I'm not that out of it. I know Carl was with me, in my office, on my desk.

"Preston, the cops—" I begin.

"Shh. We're going home now," he says, stopping me.

"You made them go away again, didn't you?" I ask, not terribly surprised.

"Everything I do is for you. You're my life. You're my angel. I'll always protect you, and I'll always be here. You can't get rid of me that easily," he says with a grin.

I smile too—a big silly smile. How does this man have this control over me? How does he have control over everyone we encounter? The cops give a wave into the room at Preston and thank him on top of it. They thanked him? Thanked him for what?

In the car I ask Preston about Brad and my parents. He says that my parents are being taken care of and that we're going to talk to Brad right now. Apparently my parents are on some sort of European vacation they won, according to Preston, but I know he sponsored the trip himself.

We pull up to the house I share with Brad, but he isn't home. Preston tells me to leave a note saying I'm leaving him and won't ever return.

"Are you kidnapping me again?" I ask.

"No, angel. I want you to be happy—not a prisoner but my equal," he says, holding my face in his hands.

After I write the note to Brad, we get into Preston's car and drive for a while. Finally we pull up into a house I don't recognize. There's a sold sign out front, and the house is completely empty. Preston tells me this is our new home—fresh to both of us and neither his nor mine but ours. He says this is our new beginning.

We spend the year getting reacquainted with each other. He's table seven again. We make love tenderly, and I like it. I'm content with tender lovemaking. He still digs deep inside me, but he'd holds my hands and tells me how much he loves me. And I truly love him. He's always beside me and always protects me. He goes on business trips, and I'm allowed to see Gwen. She still doesn't like Preston, but she says the energy around us is better.

My parents return right before the holidays, and Preston invites them over again. After they rave about how much they loved the Czech Republic, he offers to buy a house for them over there. They say they can't accept his offer, but after a little persuasion regarding the prospect that they'd never have to work again, they're sold on the idea.

My mother takes me aside and asks me if I'm truly happy. I say yes. She tells me that Brad has reached out to them. She's confused about the way I left him. She says she only wants my happiness but advises me to make amends with Brad, and I agree.

A few weeks later, Preston flies to Europe with my parents for a week to get them situated. It's their dream to live over there, and I'm so happy for them. They can always visit me, and well, they deserve it after everything I've put them through. While Preston is overseas, I decide to visit Brad at the home we once shared. I don't want Preston to get jealous over nothing, so I've waited until he was gone.

I knock on the door, and when it opens, Brad's eyes fill with tears. As he picks me up, he tells me how scared and worried he's been and adds that he thought he did something wrong. But nothing is wrong with Brad. He's perfect and kind and sweet and caring. I'm the fucked up one. I don't deserve Brad. I've always known I don't deserve him. My past is dark, and my brain is sick. I tell him I'm happy and why I don't deserve him. After I apologize for putting his health at risk with my sexual promiscuity, he says I'm the best thing that ever happened to him.

I take him out to dinner, and we eat cake at the dessert place where we tasted our wedding cake. I give his engagement ring back to him, but he insists I keep it. He asks me about the new man in my life, and I tell him it's an ex-boyfriend. When he asks about Carl, I tell him I fell out of touch with him and have no idea how he's doing. We have a few drinks then walk back to his house. I barely can stand up, and he insists I stay the night. He says he'll sleep on the couch, and I can have the bed.

The following morning, I wake up before him and kiss his forehead. I don't want to leave him the way I did before. As he opens his eyes, I hold his hands and sincerely tell him that he's the best man I've ever met and that he deserves—and will get—someone much better than me.

Leaving the house for the final time, I can't help think what my life could have been like if I had allowed myself to be happy—if I could just be content with good people in my life and accepting of good things that come my way. I'm seriously disturbed in the head—there's no question about that—and I can't have kids with Preston. In fact I can never be a functioning person in society if I don't seek help. I decide to talk to Preston about it, especially now that our sexual desires seem to have transformed into something more traditional and socially acceptable.

I walk into the house to find Preston standing there with a suitcase and a key.

"You're home early," I say, startled, confused, and happily surprised.

He grabs my arm and takes me into the guesthouse by the pool. He puts so much pressure on my arm that it's turning blue. "Preston, you're hurting me," I tell him.

He pushes me to the floor and props me up against the couch. He commands me not to move, or else he's going to knock me out. He kneels and pries up the floorboards and pops six of them out. I see a staircase and immediately know what he's going to do. "Preston, please don't do this," I plead. "Please…I don't know what I did."

He grabs hold of my throat. "Really, bitch? You don't know what you did? Whose house did you leave this morning? How many men did you fuck without a condom while you were engaged to me? After everything I've ever done for you, you're still an ungrateful little cunt."

Choking back tears, I tell him I'm sorry. "You're right, Mr. Williams. I was wrong. I'll take my punishment."

"Goddamn right, you will," he says, unzipping his pants. He turns me around and thrusts into me, just as he did at the Car Wash. My head bangs against the couch and the floor. He calls me every name in the book, and I love it; I deserve it. He asks me how many men I've slept with, and he gets off on the number. He tells me to name each one. "Glenn"—smack on the ass. "Jay"—smack to the head. "Thomas, Carradine, Quentin, Tony, Burt"—fist to the face, body slam, shake, push, spit. I love it all and want it all. I come so hard, and Preston feels it and smiles.

"This is what my baby needed. This is what my baby wanted. That's why you did all that. I know that, sweet baby," he says tenderly.

When I get into my new quarters, the place has a more modern vibe than the other one. I still have all my baby-doll dresses and lots of food. I even have my own puppy, a little chow I name "Kung Pao" 'cause he looks like a panda. Kung Pao is the only friend I know, and over time he becomes the only friend I need. When Preston goes away on his trips, I'm left in my quarters with Kung Pao and very little food. We get so skinny, but when Preston returns, he fattens us up so we'll have enough to live on the next time he leaves us.

I don't have a TV or books, and I don't get to leave my quarters like before. I sometimes ask Preston if I can have the luxury of swimming, or eating at the main house with him, but he thinks I'm playing his game and punishes me and tells me to shut up and be a whore. The lines become so blurred that I don't know what I really want anymore. Do I like being his sex slave? Or do I miss the outside world? Do I deserve this, or do I want more for myself?

Preston leaves for another trip for what seems like weeks, and I become violently ill. I don't know what to do or who to call, so I chip away at the floorboards. I chip every day for hours on end and get so fatigued that I often faint, but I know I have to get help. I think I'm dying. I sleep in between trying to break free, and Kung Pao scratches at the floorboards as well. I even catch him trying to ram his head into them. Kung Pao loves me, and that's how I know I deserve love; that's how I know I have to get out and better myself for myself but also for my parents, Kung Pao, and Preston, if he really loves me.

After weeks of clawing to get out, I finally make it through with a couple of fist punches. When I get out, I collapse immediately. I wake up to Preston shaking me, banging my body against the hardwood floor. I scream and yell and scratch at him. I tell him to stop; I'm not playing, and this is no longer a game. He continues to bash me, this time with no sexual connotation. "Are you trying to kill me?" I scream through the pain. Kung Pao is barking loudly, and I hear police sirens in the distance. The sirens draw nearer, and blood spills out of me and onto the floor.

Preston freaks out and stands up. He calls the ambulance himself just as the cops are coming into the backyard, responding to a neighbor's noise complaint. They see the blood, and they see Preston.

Preston is in a tizzy. "I don't know what happened," he says. "I don't know. I don't know what's going on. I don't know. This is my wife. This is my girlfriend, my daughter. I don't know. I don't know. Where's the ambulance?"

"Sir, calm down," one of the officers says. "You're hysterical. Help is on the way. What happened?"

Pacing back and forth, Preston replies, "I don't know" over and over.

I speak up with what little breath I have left. "I was working in my space downstairs, and I...I..."

The ambulance comes, and the paramedics treat me. Apparently I miscarried; I didn't even know I was pregnant. Preston is sobbing, crying tears the likes of which I've never seen anyone cry before. He holds me and says how sorry he is, how much he loves me and wants a family with me. "I thought this was what you wanted, Priscilla."

The ambulance takes me to the hospital so I can rest. After a few days, Preston, looking pale and thin, finally visits me. "I'm going to release you, Priscilla," he says somberly.

"Mary. My name is Mary."

"You're so special to me, but I don't deserve you," he continues.

I know his pain. "We're not good for each other."

He tells me that he got in touch with Brad and that Brad's going to meet us and take me back with him. He says Brad loves me and I love him, and he doesn't want to stand in the way of our happiness. He asks me to come back to the house one last time to get my stuff and Kung Pao and whatever else I want. Brad will be there to pick me up and take me to his house. Preston kisses my forehead and assures me that I'll be set for life and that he'll stay out of my life for good. I tell him I still want to be his friend, and then I thank him and smile.

When Preston and I pull up to the house, something seems amiss. The inside and outside lights are all off, and Kung Pao is barking wildly. When we go down to my quarters, Kung Pao's barking grows louder, and I walk in and see Brad lying facedown on the floor. I squeal and go straight to him. I feel his heart beating and am so thankful he's still alive.

"What did you do?" I yell at Preston.

"You don't want me. If I can't have you, no one can," he says, as he draws out a gun. He points it at Brad, and I beg him not to do it as I shield Brad's body with mine.

"Preston, don't do this. Please don't do this. I'll be with you forever. I'll go anywhere you want. Just don't do this."

He walks over to me and kisses me. He says we'll both be together in heaven tonight if it's God's will. He wants to end his life but also take Brad's and mine with it. At that moment I know I'm not ready to die—I want to live. I pray to God for the first time in a very long time and ask him to allow me to live. If he does, I'll do everything I can to get better.

As Preston kisses me, I feel his excitement over this new level of danger, this new level that might result in death. I never thought he'd actually want to kill me, but feeling the gun against my side now, I know it's real. As he forces his way inside me, I try to signal for Kung Pao to come over to me so I can distract Preston and get the gun away from him. Kung Pao makes his way over and bites Preston's thigh. I feel the gun move off my body and hear a gunshot that silences Kung Pao's growls.

"No!" I shriek. I become hysterical; I go out of my body and out of my mind. Seeing Kung Pao's lifeless body, I take off my heel and jam it into Preston's eyeball, causing him to release the gun that just took my best friend's life.

I have clear access to the gun but insist on taking the heel and jabbing it into every hole in his body and creating entirely new ones. I ram the heel into his other eyeball then into his throat for all those times he called me a whore. I shove it into his hands for all the times he strangled me. I don't stop there. My heel goes into his heart, his back, his thighs—any place I can find—as blood spurts onto me, into my hair, onto my baby-doll dress. This is for Kung Pao, for my unborn baby, for me.

His penis is still erect; the nasty son of a bitch is getting off on this. He's still getting off on driving me insane. Looking at my heel, I realize it isn't going to cause him enough pain. Then I look at the gun on the floor and think I'd be letting him off too easy if I shot him. What can I do to stop him from enjoying this so much?

I kneel and grab his cock. It tenses up, and I can tell he's about to come. I look at him and smile as my mouth envelops his member. He's about to explode at any second, but before he does, I take one huge bite and rip his prized package all the way off. I chew it up and spit it out. Now he's the one shaking, looking like a coward, a helpless toad. He took Kung Pao's life; he took our child's life; and he took my life.

The police show up and find Brad unconscious, Kung Pao shot and dead, and Preston, with what little life he has left, jolting periodically on the floor…and me sitting cross-legged in my baby-doll dress staring at the whole mess.

I put my fingers up to my head and mimic a gunshot. I'm too much of a coward to do it myself. The police arrest me and put me in a mental ward.

Sometimes I sit here and wonder if I was born crazy or if men made me this way—maybe not even men, maybe society. Maybe stuck-up bitches like Gwen who get whatever they want made me crazy. Perhaps it was overbearing bosses like Fat Mary who drove me to my insanity. Whoever or whatever it was, my sick brain is now being controlled. Why do movies and books glamorize sex when all it really does is ruin your life? Even the nurses and administrators try to get in my pants, knowing very well the reason I was put in here. I don't ever want to get out of here. I'm scared of what I might do to myself.

Brad visits me every once in a while. He got married. My parents told me they'd take care of me and hire at-home care for me. But they're the last people I want to hurt. I don't want to hurt anyone; I never did. It just happened. Today I'm getting interviewed for a documentary called *Maneater,* based on my story.

The interviewer walks in; he's middle-aged, with a janky haircut and a shirt two times too big. His eyes, though—his eyes are a deep chocolate brown with beautiful lashes. For the first time in a long time, my lady parts perk up. He pushes his glasses up with his nose every time he looks up at me from his notepad. He's wearing a little bow tie and a vest, and his khakis are grease stained.

He slates me and gets the lighting set up.

"Now, Miss…Oh, gosh, I'm sorry, I don't have your last name. Miss Mary—is that OK?"

"You can call me 'Coqueta,'" I say with a smile.

"Come again?" the reporter nervously asks.

I walk over to him and take off his glasses.

"It's Spanish," I state matter-of-factly, blowing my breath into his.

"Spanish for what?" he asks, his voice quavering. I reach over and feel his pants tighten up. I take my seat on his lap and giggle ever so lightly in reply to his question. "Tease," I tell him.

6542815R00053

Printed in Great Britain
by Amazon.co.uk, Ltd.,
Marston Gate.